PRAISE FOR ERIC S. BROWN

Madmen's Dreams

"From now on, whenever I'm walking down a dark hallway, I'll no longer fear the bogeyman. I'll fear the madmen behind this feverish volume."
—Eric Shapiro, author of *It's Only Temporary*

"An insane blend of horror, science fiction and military intrigue, Madmen's Dreams is an addictive feast of mind-candy sure to satisfy the most discerning of speculative fiction junkies. Eric S. Brown and D. Richard Pearce combine smart, well-crafted writing with unbound imagination to create a collection of creatures and scenarios that will linger long after the last page is turned."
—Adrienne Jones, author of *The Hoax* and *Oral Vices*

Dying Days

"*Dying Days* is a striking example of a '50s horror movie done as a short story—though without the usual happy ending."
—David Drake, author of *All the Way to the Gallows*

"Eric S. Brown has a fire in his belly and madcap devils in his fingertips. Keep an eye on this one—he'll take over the bestseller lists someday."
—Mark McLaughlin, author of *Hell Is Where The Heart Is*

Turn the page for more praise . . .

". . . for those who desire soul-searching combined with adrenaline-pumping action and suspense, *Dying Days* makes for intriguing reading."
—Alyce Wilson, *Wild Violet* magazine

"[Brown's] ability to capture the readers' imagination is powerfully magnetic."
—Steven Lloyd, *Kingdom of Shadows* (ezine)

"This is the best horror anthology that I've read in about 20 years."
—Azrael Racek, *Gothic Revue* (ezine)

Portals of Terror

"Move over King and Straub! Eric S. Brown and Angeline Hawkes-Craig are the new tag-team of horror!"
—C. Dean Andersson, author of *I Am Dracula*

"A visceral mix of pec-pumpin' horror and swoonin' snuff drama."
—Hertzan Chimera, author of *Szmonhfu* and *United States*

"This fasted-paced mixture of conjecture and fantasy tweaks the mind and keeps the adrenaline pumping. Strap yourself in and hang on for dear life."
—*Crossroads Magic* (ezine)

Still Dead

"*Still Dead* is Eric S. Brown at his cross-genre best! Nobody blends horror and science fiction quite like he does."
—C. Dennis Moore, author of *Camdigan*

Space Stations and Graveyards

". . . this book is a treat for the mind and soul. A MUST READ for those familiar with these talented writers and a GOTTA TRY for those that are not!"
—Shannon Riley, Southern Rose Productions

"There is something here for everyone. . . . Be sure to ask for this one by name!"
—Barry Hunter

ALSO BY ERIC S. BROWN

Dark Karma
Bad Mojo
Space Stations and Graveyards
Poisoned Graves
Dying Days
Flashes of Death
Blood Rain
Zombies: The War Stories
Still Dead
Portals of Terror
As We All Breakdown
Cobble (due October, 2005)

Madmen's Dreams

Eric S. Brown

With D. Richard Pearce

Edited by D.L. Snell

Permuted Press
www.permutedpress.com
Mena, AR, USA

A Permuted Press book / published by arrangement with the author

ISBN: 0-9765559-1-3

All rights reserved.
This collection © 2005 by Permuted Press

"What Rough Beast", "StarDown", "Zakku Al Rada: Aftermath", "Coughing Fits", "The Price of Arrogance", "Icy Roads", "Indigs", "Hungry", "Family", "From Heaven, into Hell", "Bad Mojo", "Fears", "A Game of Souls", "Between Two Worlds", "The Devil's Ride", "The Rising", "To Be Born", "Summer Ending", "Julie's Dream", "And The Dead Shall Rise", "Grave Watchers, Inc.", "The Last Man," "Shadows", "The Inside", "Coins", "The Underdweller", "Lucy", and "The More Things Change...," and "A Madman's Ravings" © 2004 by Eric S. Brown

"The Adversary", "The Takers", and "Jesse Wept" © 2004 by Eric S. Brown and D. Richard Pearce.

Introduction, "Hell's Daycare," and "Last One Standing" © 2004 by D. Richard Pearce.

"Inside Padded Walls" (cover art) © 2004 by Shelley Bergen.

Without limiting the rights under copyright reserved above, no part of this publication may be reproduced, stored, or introduced into a retrieval system, or transmitted, in any form, or by any means (electronic, mechanical, photocopying, recording, or otherwise), without the prior written permission of both copyright owner and the above publisher of this book.

Table of Contents

Introduction (by D. Richard Pearce) — 9
What Rough Beast — 11
StarDown — 16
And The Dead Shall Rise — 18
The Adversary (with D. Richard Pearce) — 22
Zakku Al Rada: Aftermath — 39
Coughing Fits — 43
The Price of Arrogance — 47
Icy Roads — 50
Indigs — 53
Hungry — 58
Family — 60
From Heaven, Into Hell — 65
Bad Mojo — 68
Fears — 70
A Game of Souls — 72
Between Two Worlds — 74
The Devil's Ride — 77
The Rising — 79
To Be Born — 81
Summer Ending — 83
Julie's Dream — 85
Grave Watchers, Inc. — 88
The Last Man — 91
Shadows — 93
The Inside — 96
Coins — 99
Loose — 101
The Takers (with D. Richard Pearce) — 105
Jesse Wept (with D. Richard Pearce) — 111
The Under-dweller — 117
Lucy — 121
The More Things Change — 124
Hell's Daycare (by D. Richard Pearce) — 126
Last One Standing (by D. Richard Pearce) — 137
A Madman's Ravings — 156

Introduction

Writers have colossal egos.

This probably doesn't come as a surprise to anyone reading this, though you may be surprised to hear someone (especially a writer) actually say it. The fact is, any writer is simply a person who has read something and thought, "Hey, I can tell it better than that," or, "That was pretty good, but I would have done this . . . " or, even when reading their favorite author, "I can do that." Even if the writer uses a pseudonym, as I do (I'm also an editor and publisher, and feel the need to differentiate), it's still about the ego—I know who D. Richard Pearce is; whether you're praising or slamming him, it's still my ego.

Which makes you wonder how in the world people could ever collaborate on a story.

Well, it ain't easy. Fortunately, good writers know the give and take of sharing and trading info, and they know the value of constructive criticism. Often, a comment from a reader or editor will not only make sense, but will also resonate further than intended. So when collaborations happen, if both writers are reasonable people, a story can only get better as it goes. And then you have two (or more) egos to stroke.

Whew.

Speaking of that second ego, Eric S. Brown is a good writer. In terms of words, he's one of the most amazing people I've ever seen—he has the ability to sit down and pound out words in a way that makes me very jealous. In something like three years, he has pounded out more stories than I will write in my life—I know this, and it's okay. I'm slow and meticulous; he gets them out there and lets them play. Sometimes there's room for change, and he's okay with that. It's what makes him a good collaborative writer.

Within these pages, you'll find many stories from Eric, a couple from me, and a few from both of us. I'm sure that you will see the stylistic differences, and you may favor one over the other. That's okay, too—readers' tastes are as broad as writers' styles, and hey, love makes the world go 'round, viva la diference, etcetera, ad nauseum.

For my part, I find that some of my favorite creations lie within these pages—and I think my best collaborative effort lives in here, too. Lucky you.

Oh—sorry. That was just my ego talking.

—D. Richard Pearce

What Rough Beast

Clint sat on the porch of the Mom and Pop gas station. The summer heat was almost unbearable, and sweat glistened on his chest. The only clothing he wore was a loose pair of boxer shorts. The swinging bench he rested on creaked as he used his bare feet to rock back and forth. Clint stared out into the empty highway and barren sand that stretched for miles in both directions.

He'd lived here almost two months now, ever since he'd paused during his desperate flight from the city and had found the old man lying on the porch with half his face gone and a high-powered rifle clutched in his rigid hands. *This*, Clint had thought, *must be Pop.*

After a whole hour of stuffing himself on the gas station's groceries, Clint finally found Mom. Apparently, she had died before Pop, and the old man had locked her away in the store's cellar sometime before taking his own life. He hadn't had the heart to deal with her.

When Clint had heard the bumping and shuffling from the cellar, he'd put two and two together and grabbed his 9mm from his car. Even armed, he'd had a close call. When he unlocked the door, Mom broke out so fast that Clint had to put five rounds in her chest just to keep her away long enough to get a clean headshot. He vomited long and hard over her decomposing corpse before carrying her outside and burying her behind the station, alongside Pop.

As Clint had shoveled, he realized just how much fortune had smiled on him. The station, also a general store and a home for its owners, had its own food, water, fuel, and even a generator. Best of all, it was in the middle of nowhere. He'd ended up staying the night there and then had simply decided to stay.

He took what he felt were the necessary precautions: he locked and boarded up all the windows and the backdoor, leaving only the heavy wooden main door and its screen unfortified so he could come and go as he pleased. He'd also moved a good portion of the station's supplies into the cellar should he be forced to retreat into its depths. But he had also filled his gas tank and moved his car as close to the station's main door as he could, just in case. It was better to be prepared for everything than to be left wanting. Yet in the time that he'd stayed at the station, he'd only seen one car streak by. He had run outside to flag the driver down, but the car had disappeared over the horizon. There had been no sign of the dead, and he thanked the lord for it every night.

At first, he'd spent his time listening to the radio because the station had no TV. The airwaves had been filled with civilian newscasters nearly screaming about the "dead plague" and about how the urban areas had became deathtraps due to their heavy populations. These rants had been sharply contrasted by the calm fronts of military guests and guests from the Center for Disease Control, who were on the shows constantly these days. It seemed that no one really knew what was happening. The dead had just started refusing to die, and the living were paying the price. The dead roamed the streets, killing everyone they came across, victims rising to join their ranks.

By Clint's third day in his new home, the radio stations began to vanish from the airwaves, one by one. His hopes of humanity getting it together and beating this disaster started to grow dark. Then, on the fourth day, the first radio station came back on the air. That had been the moment all Clint's hope of rescue had died. The show had been the same and yet startlingly different. The DJ's voice was hollow, and it grated like boots on gravel. His slow jagged speech was not human in any way, and at random intervals he began to speak in a language unlike any Clint had ever heard, a series of hisses and clicks that caused Clint to shudder inside. By the end of his first week at the gas station, Clint had taken the radio outside and had blown it to bits with the old man's rifle.

Clint spent the rest of his time in utter isolation except for the company of a lone coyote that came out from the sands at dark to rummage through the trash in search of food. As time went by, Clint and his visitor forged a mutually beneficial relationship. Clint began to leave out food, and eventually the coyote would let him sit on the porch and talk to it as it ate and nosed through the trash for more.

Back on the porch, Clint reached up and wiped the sweat from his brow. He took a sip from the can of hot Coke in his hand and got up from the bench. The sun was beginning to set, and he wanted to get ready for his friend. But as he turned to head inside, he saw smoke.

Clint blinked and shook his head, trying to clear it. In the distance, a cloud of thick, black smoke billowed up towards the heavens. Clint wondered for a moment how long it had been there. Had he been so lost in his own mind that he hadn't noticed it before, or had it simply risen up as he had gotten off the bench? Part of him wanted to pretend it wasn't there at all, to simply head back into the station and go on with his routine, but he knew he couldn't. If people were out there, they might need his help, or perhaps they might be able to help him. And if it were the dead, coming for him at last, he needed to know so that he could prepare.

He dressed in the clothes that he'd arrived in, packed a bag with water and a first aid kit, and checked the old man's rifle: it was fully loaded, so he swung it onto his shoulder by the carrying strap. Clint had ruled out taking the car to investigate. The noise of its engine would give him away for sure, and if it were the dead, they would flock to him in droves, even if he ran. They'd follow him back here, and he would be forced to run again. The station still had enough stock to keep him going for months if rationed properly, and he had no intentions of giving it up easily. So he set out on foot towards the smoke, miles away to the south.

After an hour's walk, Clint stood on the sand and stared at the wreck up ahead of him through a pair of binoculars that he'd looted from the store. The smoke was coming from an overturned eighteen-wheeler. The gas tank had exploded at some point after the massive truck had run off the road and overturned, and small blazes still leapt and danced about in its wreckage. Three people, two men and a woman, moved about on the road near it. It appeared as if they were arguing over something which lay in the middle of the road between them, though it was not clear if they had survived the accident or not. The dead acted so much like the breathing until you got too close and they saw you.

Silently, Clint crept through the dunes towards the trio. As he drew nearer, he could see that one of the men carried a high-powered hunting rifle like his own, but the others appeared unarmed. Clint lifted his binoculars again, focusing on the dark lump in the asphalt that they seemed to be fighting over. As he recognized it, bile rose up in his throat. It was—correction, had been—his friend. The coyote's body was a crumpled mass of shattered bones from its midsection down, but its front end was intact, though smeared with blood.

As he watched it snarl and snap at the people around it, Clint could hear its tortured yipping inside his mind, calling to him, calling *for* him. He was able to see the people clearly now, and there was no doubt that they were alive, battered and bruised and looking terribly underfed, but alive.

Clint started to get to his feet and run to them just as the man raised the rifle and leveled it at the coyote's head. Clint's instinct took over. He dropped back to one knee and jerked his own rifle up, taking aim. The night cracked with thunder, and the man's lifeless body toppled to the road with a hole between its eyes. Everything seemed to move in a blur. The woman screamed. Clint was running to them. His 9mm was suddenly in his hand. A series of shots echoed again. When the redness cleared from Clint's vision, he found himself among his victim's bodies, watching blood leak slowly onto the road from the woman's unmoving lips.

His friend, the coyote, snarled at him with hunger, and maggots swarmed through its coarse fur. He looked into its eyes and felt tears sliding down his own cheeks.

The unarmed man he'd just put three rounds into moments before began to twitch and stir with un-life.

Surrounded by the dead and the true dead alike, Clint finally gave up. The barrel of his 9mm scratched the roof of his mouth. And as the coyote continued to yip and drag itself towards him, Clint shut his eyes and squeezed the trigger.

StarDown

Being sick sucked big time. Being sick and on the run was worse. Jake lay propped up against the hotel's bathroom wall. The whole room stunk of blood. The toilet seat was raised, and red streaks still dripped down the sides of the porcelain. He could feel the tiny tentacles moving around inside of him, squirming and trying to find a way out.

Jake stared down at the pistol on the tiles beside him and wondered why he had bothered to run in the first place. Deep down, he had known he didn't really have a chance, even as he'd put a bullet through his partner's face. He had disappeared into the night long before the containment and clean-up crew had arrived.

For the last five years, Jake had been the StarDown project's top boy. He was something of a living legend inside the black-op agency. He'd traveled across the globe and put in check dozens of attempts at full-scale colonization by the "squids." Hundreds of people—the infected, those who were unlucky enough to get in his way, and those who knew too much—had met death at the barrel of his gun. There were times when he felt guilt over his past, but he needed only to remember the nature of the squids, the threat they posed to the whole human race, and the guilt would evaporate into the mists of his mind.

It was said that to truly understand the squids, one had to see a nest. He'd torched quite a few in his time, and those memories haunted him: their numbers growing until a mass of tentacled horrors, each no larger than a man's hand, burst the host and poured out in search of a fresh body, a fresh breeding ground; their razor-sharp scales glistening with the blood of their host. All it took was the slightest scratch, a single alien cell entering your bloodstream, and it was the end of the road.

Jake ran his thumb over the healing wound on his wrist. Yes, he had known full well what he was doing when he had splattered agent Henderson's brain matter onto the passenger side window of the StarDown car. He knew that if she had turned him in, it would have meant his death. There was no cure for the squid parasites, but one in every ten thousand humans was supposed to be immune to infection. Approximately. He only wanted the time to see if he fell in that narrow minority.

Three hours had passed since he'd murdered Henderson. He knew StarDown operatives would be here soon. No one could run or hide from an agency like StarDown for long, not even an insider like himself. But he knew now that he was going to die either way, and he hoped they found him before the squids split him open and poured out onto the tile, crawling into the hotel in search of new hosts. It was far too late for suicide, and he didn't have the strength to lift his gun, anyway. Jake leaned back, closed his eyes, and prayed for those in the neighboring hotel rooms . Then, his body went into spasms and the blackness overtook him like clouds of ink.

And The Dead Shall Rise

Chris ducked farther into the brush surrounding the road as the police cruiser slowed. An officer leaned out of the passenger window, shining a hand lamp across the tree line. Maggots slithered in and out of his pale, rotting cheeks.

Chris held his breath and prayed that his luck would hold. The light moved over his face, burning his eyes—and moved on past him into the trees.

"Nothing here," the officer said in the hollow, cold voice of the dead. The cruiser picked up speed and disappeared over the nearby hill.

Chris started to breathe again, mopping at the sweat on his brow with the sleeve of his filthy and tattered flannel shirt. It had been close, too close. Only God knew what would've happened had the officers discovered him. Chris had heard stories that the last "Breathers" were being herded up, gathered into breeding centers so that they weren't forced completely into extinction as the society of the dead took their place as the rulers of the Earth.

Everything had changed so much over the past year; Chris still wondered if he were stuck inside one of his own nightmares. In the before times, he had been a powerful man, the owner of a chain of grocery stores that stretched from one coast of America to the other. He'd had women, money, respect, but none of that mattered now. Like anyone else left alive, he was merely food—an animal to be hunted and killed.

Chris jumped out of the brush onto the road and ran off in the opposite direction that the cruiser had gone. His breath came in ragged gasps as he pushed his body beyond its limits. He remembered the days when the dead were slow, pitiful things, lumbering around like mindless automatons. If only the world had awoken sooner to the danger they posed, they'd never have been allowed to evolve into what they were. Now, they spoke, drove cars, used weapons and did all the things Breathers used to.

Chris had not seen another living soul in weeks, and he didn't know how much longer he could go on. He felt so very tired. The past few months, he'd managed to survive more through luck than skill.

Chris came to a jarring halt in the middle of the road as he saw a house up ahead. There were lights on inside, and smoke rolled out of its rock chimney towards the stars. Chris was not naive enough to believe that there could be real people inside, but a gnawing curiosity made him approach it.

He ducked off the side of the road into the trees and crept towards the house's lawn. He could see someone or something moving above the sink through the kitchen window. Chris sank to his belly. He dug his .38 revolver from his jacket pocket, carrying it openly as he crawled across the dark yard.

He reached the side of the house and got to his feet, leaning against the wall, careful to stay out of view of the window. He could hear the sounds of leftovers being scraped off a plate into the sink. Chris snuck around the side of the house, searching for another window, wanting desperately to get a look inside.

The lights were off in the living room as he peeked through its window; only the dim glow of a TV screen lit the room. A man sat in a recliner, watching the screen intently. The man's flesh was gray and decayed. At his feet sat a young boy. The child paid no attention to the TV, staring directly out the window at Chris.

Chris jumped back as if he'd been physically struck, but when no alarm sounded from within the house, he found the nerve to peer inside once more. Then he noticed the boy's eyes. He looked into the child's empty sockets and watched as a worm worked its way free and fell to the wooden floor.

The tiny child began to cry. The man in the recliner yelled something that Chris couldn't quite make out and got to his feet. He scooped the child up in his arms and yelled again. A woman entered the room from the kitchen, her long blonde hair matted to her scalp with blood and pus from an ancient wound on her forehead. She rested her hands on her hips and scowled at the man. Chris thought he heard her say something about bedtime.

Chris ducked below the window. The woman, despite being dead, had eyes that still saw. He remained motionless until the voices disappeared deeper into the house.

Chris felt sick. Leaning over, he nearly vomited onto the grass. He'd never imagined that the dead could really live like this. They were supposed to be monsters-hungry evil things waiting to tear the flesh off your bones. Not a mother and father tucking their child in for the night.

Crowning the hill with bright lights, the police cruiser was heading back toward Chris and the house. He stood in plain view of the road and there was no way he could cross the distance to the trees before the cruiser reached the house.

Inside his mind, whatever remnants of surviving sanity gave way. He charged out onto the road in front of the cruiser, shouting at the top of his lungs.

"Jesus!" the officer at the wheel screamed as he swerved to the left, narrowly avoiding Chris. His partner snatched up the car radio. "This is car 71. We have a Breather down by the Peterson farm on route 106. Requesting back-up!"

Chris aimed and fired several times at the thing behind the wheel. The windshield shattered, spraying shards of glass into the car as the bullets tore into the officer's chest. The thing leapt out of the car as goo leaked from the wounds, blackening the front of its uniform. "Drop your weapon!" it shouted, pointing its own handgun at Chris.

Chris turned to flee back towards the house as the front door swung open. The father-creature stood there with a 12 gauge leveled at Chris's stomach. He saw his own fear and hatred reflected in the thing's dull, glazed eyes. The night shook as the 12 gauge thundered. The blast knocked Chris off his feet, his intestines spilling onto the dirt as he fell.

The officer ran over to stand above him, pointing his pistol into Chris's face. Chris smelt the officer's ripe state of decay as black pus dripped from its wounds onto his face. The last thing Chris saw was the barrel exploding with light milliseconds before the bullet ripped through his brain.

The mother-thing ran out of the house, shoving her husband aside as she made her way onto the lawn. "Oh God!" she wailed, seeing Chris's corpse sprawled before her. Blood dripped from Chris's forehead onto the asphalt as his body twitched, growing cold.

The officer turned to her, a smile on his withered lips. "It's all right ma'am. Everything's okay. The monster's dead now."

The Adversary

The morning was dark and cold. Rain fell from the black clouds, and Dan could hear the wind howling over the patrol car's engine. He sat in the driver's seat, casting impatient glances at Johnson's gas station. Alex had insisted they stop for coffee, but Dan knew it was just an excuse for him to see Sheena. She always worked the morning shift, and Alex had it bad for her.

Dan lit a cigarette, but kept his window rolled up. If Alex could waste their time like this, he could damn well smoke in the car.

The car's radio crackled to life with Maxine's voice: "Dan? You there?"

Dan sighed and reluctantly picked up the radio. "Yeah. What's up?"

"Mark just called, Dan. He's got some kind of problem over at the construction site where they're building the new school. He wouldn't say what it was, but he seemed kind of shook up. He wants you out there ASAP."

"Can't you just send Harry?"

"Sorry, Dan. Mark asked for the sheriff, not a deputy. He was rather frantic."

"Damn it, Max, it's probably just another worker dispute."

"Watch your language," Maxine ordered sternly. "Just go see what he wants."

"Yes ma'am. We're on it." Dan slammed the radio back onto the dash as Alex opened the passenger door. He carried a cardboard tray holding two steaming cups. His smile turned to a frown as he saw Dan's face. He climbed into the car, shutting the door as he glared at Dan's cigarette. "I thought you were going to quit."

Dan shrugged and flipped on the siren, gunning the car out of the station's parking lot.

"Jesus!" Alex wailed, trying to keep the coffee from scalding his groin as it sloshed around in his lap. "What the hell's your problem?"

"Mark's got some kind of trouble out at the construction site again."

"And that's got you this pissed off?"

Dan didn't answer. The drive to the construction site was silent except for Alex's feigned coughing at Dan's second-hand smoke.

As they pulled into the site for Bethel County's new school, the lot was nearly vacant. Only Mark's pickup and a few unattended "diggers" were around. None of the usual workers were to be seen. The place appeared totally dead except for the light in Mark's office trailer.

Dan marched up the small entrance ramp to Mark's trailer and started to knock. Mark jerked the door open so quickly that Dan was caught in mid-knock. Mark's face was pale. His normal know-it-all cocky attitude had been replaced by a look of fear. "Thank God, Sheriff. I'm glad you're here. Come on inside." He talked so fast that Dan's head swam.

Dan and Alex entered the trailer as Mark shut the door behind them. Mark's office was a mess of jumbled papers, a desk, two oddly placed chairs, and blueprints stapled all over the walls.

"So what's going on, Mark?" Dan asked, plopping into one of the chairs. Mark stared at him as if searching for words. "Well, Sheriff, as you know, we're trying to build the county's new school here."

Dan nodded, tapping his fingers on the desk.

"We're laying the foundations now."

"Get to the point, Mark," Dan ordered.

"This morning we were doing some blasting, getting rid of the last rocks we couldn't move, and we found . . . I don't know what we found . . . But I sent the men home. I called you right off, Sheriff, because I've never seen anything like it."

"Like what?" Alex asked. "What did you find?"

Mark struggled to keep his composure. "I think you need to see it for yourselves or you'll never believe it." Mark picked up a pair of heavy flashlights and handed one to Dan. "Come on."

Outside, the drizzle had worked into a full-fledged rain. Mark led them across the site to the edge of a large hole in the middle of where the foundation was being laid. The stench coming out of the hole was so strong that Alex actually did start coughing. Dan made a face of disgust. The smell was unmistakable, putrid and rotting. Dan knew what he would find before he even turned the beam of his flashlight into the hole, though he had no idea it would be so many. The pale beam traced its way over arms and legs, dozens upon dozens of rotting corpses packed the hole like sardines.

"My God," Dan muttered. "How many do you think are in there?"

"Don't know," Mark shrugged, looking green and on the verge of vomiting. "I'd say at least two hundred."

"Two hundred," Alex echoed, shaking his head.

"You see why I called you, Sheriff? I...I can't deal with this. I'm just an engineer."

And barely that, thought Dan, but he said, "Go on home. Nothing for you to do here. I'm betting there isn't going to be a school built here now."

Mark sputtered an incoherent protest, looked at the pit again, and then bolted for his pick-up. Dan was sure the bastard was just as glad to be gone as he was to see him go.

"D . . .Dan?" Alex asked.

He turned to look at his trembling deputy. Alex had dropped his coffee and stood staring in shock at the pit. "What do we do?"

"Call for backup."

An hour later, the site was crawling with cops, medics, rescue workers, journalists, and even a pair of SBI men.

The Feds were still on their way. Body after body had been hauled from the pit; all naked with their bones so crushed they looked like human putty. Men, women, children . . . Dan had never seen anything like it. He wondered where he'd put them all. The town morgue and the hospital combined couldn't handle this many. In the end, he guessed it wouldn't really be his problem. Agent Jeffery Thompson of the SBI had already taken over the situation, and for all Dan cared, he could have it. Dan was forced to admit this was out of his league.

Dan had sent Alex home earlier. The poor kid just hadn't been able to cope with this and got in the way more than he helped.

Dan bit into a sandwich that the volunteers from the local fire department had provided and leaned against his patrol car. The sandwich was already stale, and he threw it aside. So much for breakfast. He thought about going over to Mark's trailer, where Agent Thompson had set up a makeshift base of operations, to tell the SBI prick that he had enough and was going home, but then he thought better of it. No point antagonizing the state—he might just get assigned a grunt task.

Sudden warmth in his hand made him look down. Blood was dripping from his clenched fist. He opened his left hand and frowned. It didn't hurt, but he must have been clenching so hard he'd driven his nails right into the palm. He glanced back at the hole and shook his head. This shit didn't make sense. He wrapped a handkerchief around his hand and headed for his car.

As he drove, he kept rolling over in his mind how something like this could happen in Bethel—middle-of-nowhere Bethel, North Carolina. Small towns were supposed to be immune to this kind of shit. He'd moved here after serving as a cop in New York to get away from the crime and the horrors of the big city. Well, that and there weren't a lot of Catholics around here.

He felt sick, a lump in his throat. *Too many smokes and not enough food*, he reckoned.

Two hundred bodies in an unexplainable mass grave, all crushed, all only days old if their appearance told the truth—how in God's name does something like that happen? There was no way someone could haul that many bodies into Bethel, much less find the time to dig a mass grave for them at a place like the construction site. Someone would have seen *something*. If not the workers, then someone driving by on the main road. It always stayed busy even at night since it was the only road in and out of town that connected to an interstate.

As Dan pulled into the gravel driveway at the end of his yard, a black sedan sat waiting for him. He noticed it had out-of-state tags and guessed the Feds had finally showed—funny that they weren't using a Government Issue car, though. They'd have questions for him, more than he could stomach at this point. A man sat behind the sedan's wheel and glanced at Dan as he parked. He wore a causal blue jacket over a white shirt and looked to be in his twenties.

As Dan got out, the man walked around the car to greet him. "Sheriff Jackson?" he asked.

"You a Fed? They send you down here to make my life even more of a living hell?"

The man smiled. "No. My name is Darven. I am with the church."

"The church?" Dan said. "What church?"

Darven appeared to be a bit insulted. "The Church. The one in Rome."

Dan slammed the car door and made for his porch. "Get the hell off my land before I arrest you for trespassing! I've dealt with enough assholes and whackos today already!"

Darven took a step and grabbed Dan by the arm. "Sheriff, I strongly suggest you hear me out. If you don't, I cannot be held responsible for the repercussions."

Dan tore free of Darven's grasp. "Look mister, in case you didn't know, we just uncovered a mass grave today, two hundred people dead and rotting in the ground. I'm not exactly in the mood to talk about God."

"Nor I, Sheriff," Darven went on, "but you need to know what you found. We must act quickly. Those people weren't dead. They weren't even human."

Dan stopped for a moment. This guy was certifiable, all right. "Father, or whatever you have exactly five seconds to be out of here before I start shooting."

Darven started to protest, but saw the graveness in Dan's eye. Maybe grave enough to carry out his threat. He glanced at Dan's makeshift bandage, and his eyes narrowed, but he turned and got into his car.

He was gone before Dan was inside.

On the TV, the Asheville station was showing a breaking story. Sources were tight-lipped, but reports estimated that as many as thirty-five corpses were being pulled from the proposed site of the new school in Bethel. Causes of death were unknown, but foul play was definitely suspected.

"Thirty-five?" Dan was a little surprised they had even admitted that number, but he supposed it would be hard for the state guys to hide the huge numbers coming out of that pit. Common practice though; the truth would just cause a panic situation, as everyone with a missing person in the family would be trying to get info out of the state, or the feds, if they ever got here. With the public becoming inured to the track records of serial killers, thirty-five was just a curiosity, not a record.

Dan contemplated going to bed, but didn't think he'd be able to sleep. He half-dozed on the couch as the news continued with speculation and interviews with press decoys, state and local. His mind wandered to the pit. He had seen some pretty brutal stuff during his time in New York, first as a kid in Brooklyn, then later as a beat cop. Blood, violence and death—none of it was new to him, and scale didn't really make it much different.

The burning question for the state was who were all those people and how did they get down there? But something else bothered Dan.

He had watched the retrieval of the corpses for a while, and had played a game that he hadn't had to play since Brooklyn. He watched the faces of the corpses as they came out of the pit, and made up stories about them. He used to do that to help him remember that these were people, not just case numbers. He'd imagine a kid playing basketball with his buddies, imagine the smile of a woman making dinner while her body was being carted off. It was hard on him, but it kept it real, kept him from becoming desensitized to violent death.

As he had watched this morning though, something hadn't been right. The eyes of the dead had looked back. He hadn't been able to make up any stories. Since the corpses were all naked and mass buried, there were no clues to go by, no Nike sneakers to play basketball in, no jeans or hairclips or anything. And the gazes of these dead weren't vacant; they seemed to be looking directly at him, assessing him. The dead seemed to almost recognize him. They looked at him as though they should know him, but couldn't place him.

He had shaken it off at the time, thought he was just overwhelmed by the sheer magnitude of this crime and by the fact that he was no longer used to seeing death so prominently displayed. Their gazes, now that he had time to think about it, reminded him of his mother. She had looked the same way.

Dan had been born and raised in Brooklyn, by his grandparents. His grandmother was a devout Catholic, his grandfather a good man, but indifferent to God. Dan's mother had been autistic and had never left home. She had become pregnant at twenty-four, but Dan never had any idea who his father was. His mother had died giving birth to him, but he used to talk to her picture, and the look in her eyes, that faint recognition, was always there.

"We followed you, we believed you," they said, melding together and apart again. "You betrayed us. We have been waiting for you." Dan awoke suddenly with the corpses screaming at him. Someone was banging on the door.

Dan tried to shake the sleep out of his mind as he stumbled into the front room. He was drenched in sweat. No, not sweat. He swiped at his forehead, and his hands were covered in blood. He glanced at the couch—there was blood all over it.

The door banged again. "Just a second!" he yelled, heading for the bathroom. He splashed water on his face and wiped down quickly. He couldn't see where he was bleeding, and it seemed to have stopped.

"Dan! Open up!" Alex sounded frantic. Dan jerked the door open and Alex barged in; the rain was coming down in buckets.

"Why didn't you answer your phone?" Alex asked.

Dan glanced around. "Um, I guess I didn't hear it. What time is it?"

"Eight o'clock."

"Really? Wow, I must have been bagged. Want some dinner?"

"It's eight in the morning, Dan!"

The sheriff was stunned: he'd just slept nearly twenty hours. "Oh. So what's going on at the site?"

"Sheriff, are you okay?"

"Fine. Why?"

"Because the whole county's going ape-shit is why. Those corpses are alive."

Dan's head reeled. Alex looked around and saw the bloodstained couch. "Dan, I mean it, are you all right?"

"Alex, I think I'm the one who should be asking that. What do you mean *alive*?"

"I mean *alive*. They finally got them all out. They made the ER into a morgue and then took over the gym at the high school. There's two hundred and fifty-three altogether. Examiners have been brought in from all over the state. At four o'clock, one started breathing. Now, most of them have vital signs."

"Holy shit."

Alex nodded. "And then some. Thompson's been frothing at the mouth, wondering where you are, and the feds are here now. He's mostly been bumped, but they want to talk to you."

"I don't know anything they don't."

Alex shrugged. "I know, but they still want you there. Big dog's a guy named Mendelson, from Washington. And they have a priest or something, consulting. He keeps asking for you."

Damn it, thought Dan. *Fucking church*. After what they had put his grandparents through... "All right," he said. "Let's go."

Alex drove while Dan smoked, deep in thought. He tried to remember what he had blocked so long ago, tried to recall everything about the church that he could. He knew for sure that his grandparents had been banned from the church, formally excommunicated because of him.

He knew that a priest had molested him, or tried, and that the priest had committed suicide. He was very young at the time, but there was a big stink about the whole thing. After his grandmother died a couple years later, he and his grandfather had moved into an apartment in another neighborhood. But the rumors followed them.

Alex screeched into the hospital parking lot, slowing a bit as a soldier halted them. He was still rolling when he yelled to the soldier: "I have the sheriff. Mendelson wants him!"

The soldier waved him through.

Dan turned in his seat, looking back. "National Guard?"

"You know it, Sheriff. Governor thinks we got us an Armageddon."

They went in the hospital main doors, past more soldiers, state police and agents. Alex led Dan to the administration office, where Mendelson had moved the base of operations.

As they entered the office, two more agents stopped them at the door. "This is Sheriff Jackson," said Alex. They checked Dan's ID and sent him in

"Ah. Sheriff Jackson, I presume." Mendelson was a balding man, short and sweaty with a respectable middle-age spread. He looked more like an algebra teacher than a federal agent.

"Fuck you," said Dan good-naturedly.

Mendelson was surrounded by three more Feds, a couple of state guys (not counting Thompson, who was pouting), and Darven.

Dan said, "I know when I'm over my head, and I knew if you needed me, you'd call. Looks like you've got plenty of help here."

Mendelson grinned, and Dan found it hard to hate him. "Good. I'm glad you're not another one of these backwoods cowboys. And you're right. Ordinarily, I'd send you on vacation, but your presence was requested by Father Darven here. And now, I don't think anything will happen 'ordinarily' for awhile."

Dan ignored the priest, who looked at him earnestly, almost hungrily, and focused on Mendelson. "What's the priest doing here?"

Mendelson shrugged. "Father Darven is an expert consultant from the Vatican. He was leading a conference in Washington and was passing through Bethel when our shit hit the fan. He has very graciously agreed to help us in this matter."

Bullshit, thought Dan, but he said, "What kind of consultant?"

"Father Darven is an exorcist."

Dan looked at Mendelson, but he didn't think he was kidding. "What exactly is the situation?"

"I'm sure your deputy filled you in on the way over here. We have two hundred and fifty-three corpses, or former corpses, I suppose, in various states of decomposition. Their bodies are intact, but their skeletons appear to be crushed. All of the corpses were exhumed before we began examination at approximately 0330 this morning. At 0405, the first corpse began breathing, and at present, we have one hundred and forty nine corpses—" he broke off as an agent poked her head in the door, holding up two fingers, "—make that one hundred and fifty one corpses with vital signs."

"That's impossible."

"Yes, Sheriff, it is. But...I'd appreciate it if you kept what I'm about to say under your hat. We don't have a fucking clue what to do."

Dan sighed, still not sure why he was here. "You think an exorcist is going to help?"

Mendelson laughed, "I'm Jewish, Sheriff. But I'll take any help I can get at this point."

"You think I can help?"

The fed pointed at Darven. "He does."

Dan sighed again. "All right, priest. What do you want to know?"

Darven started, a troubled look on his face. "I wish you had spoken with me yesterday, Daniel. I would have kept this confidential, but we're running out of time."

"Say what you have to say, but I am not Daniel to you or your pack of wolves. If you address me, call me Sheriff."

Darven nodded. "Very well, Sheriff. You are Daniel Jackson, correct? Grandson of Harold and Mabel Jackson, of Brooklyn, New York?"

Dan bristled at the priest's tone, but nodded.

The priest continued. "You are stigmatic, and you have performed miracles."

The room was silent, as all eyes turned to the sheriff. His head swam, but he managed to murmur, "I don't know what you're talking about..."

"Yes, Sheriff, you do. When you were six, one of our priests tried to touch you, and you threw him out of a fourth story window. You bled as a child, bled with the wounds of Christ."

The others in the room were unreadable, except for Thompson, who smirked, and except for Alex, who was staring at Dan in horror.

"We've kept track of you since the excommunication, which was largely due to your grandfather threatening to go public with the unfortunate Father Isol's...indiscretion. We have made some mistakes, granted, but we always kept track of you, Daniel."

Dan rallied his shaking nerves. "I don't know what you're talking about, priest." He turned to Mendelson. "You're not taking this clown seriously, are you?" But Dan was betrayed by his own hands, which both started to bleed.

Thompson stopped smirking, and Mendelson said simply, "We have to know what it all means, Sheriff. And you're the closest thing to a saint we have."

They donned hazardous material gear borrowed from the fire station and entered the gym, where a dozen medical examiners were making the rounds of the corpses. The examiners were attired in HAZMAT body suits from the CDC.

They communicated through microphones in the headpieces.

"These aren't human bodies, gentlemen. They are the seraphim, angels if you will, who followed Lucifer when he was hurled from Heaven. They landed on the earth millennia ago, and were eventually covered by the earth itself. But we have uncovered them, and now they wake from their slumber." Darven's voice droned on in their headsets.

Dan glanced at Alex, and twirled his finger next to his head.

Alex flashed a wan smile, but his eyes held fear and distrust. Dan sighed.

"Doubtless, the Adversary will want these angels, perhaps come for them as he begins to gather an army, to start the end times."

"Or maybe they're aliens," said Dan into the headset. "Mendelson, you can't tell me that this guy is stamped with government approval."

"Just following orders, cowboy. The big guys don't know what these freaks are, but they're not taking any chances. What do your saint powers tell you?"

"That I need a beer, a burger, and a shave, and not necessarily in that order."

"Cowboy," Mendelson's voice was firm now, "you have to admit something's going on here. If inspiration hits you please, for the love of God, don't fight it."

Suddenly there was a muffled scream from across the ER. One of the corpses sat up and with a negligent gesture, casually ripped a medical examiner in two.

Yells and curses filled the headsets as agents drew their guns and opened fire on the corpse. Their gunshots didn't even phase the creature, which seemed vaguely male. He had some trouble with his locomotion, and seemed almost to slither towards them.

The priest stepped forward, brandishing his cross, and began to chant a sacred text in Latin. The creature paused in front of him, flashing a crooked smile. It spoke with a dusty voice: "Your words cannot harm me, cross-man. I see the betrayer standing before me." He looked past the priest, who was still frantically chanting, straight at Dan.

Blood filled Dan's visor, and he felt suffocated. He tore the thing off, wiping blood off his brow. He aimed his gun straight at the head. "What do you want from me?"

"What we have always wanted, since the beginning. We followed you, and you left us. We have waited. It is time." So saying, he lifted Father Darvin off the floor. The corpse's jaw unhinged like that of a snake and bit the priest's head off.

Alex turned, heaving into his helmet, and the rest of them opened fire on the creature. Mendelson was screaming for the rest of the examiners to evacuate the building as more of the creatures began to stir.

As soon as the examiners were out, Mendelson ordered a retreat. The creature came on, their bullets still not phasing it. As they went out the door, soldiers were rushing in, wielding flamethrowers and grenade launchers.

The flames seemed to slow the creature, which retreated toward the far wall. But it didn't ignite. In the hallway, Mendelson cast an accusing look at Dan. "Well?"

Dan shook his head. "I...I don't know."

"Well, you better think of something. *Now*. Get your man outside."

Dan grabbed Alex, and Mendelson called the Guard back. Once outside, Mendelson ordered the building destroyed. "Keep launching grenades into that motherfucker," he told the captain of the guard. "I want smoking rubble in ten minutes."

Dan was helping Alex get out of his suit when Mendelson approached them. He signaled Dan, and walked away.

"It recognized you," said the Fed as Dan approached.

"Mendelson..."

"Are you a religious man?" When Dan shook his head, Mendelson continued, "Well, if what that priest said was true, I can understand why not. Listen to me a minute, though. There is some weird shit going on around here."

"Can't argue with that." Dan grinned, despite the apocalyptic setting. Explosions rattled through the air.

"Your priest in there, he thought those things were fallen angels, and if that's so, then what does that make you?"

"I'm not a saint, Mendelson."

"Just the opposite, is what I'm thinking. That...*thing* recognized you, called you the betrayer. Who'd you betray?"

"Jesus, Mendelson, are you saying I'm the Antichrist now?"

The Fed shook his head, "I don't know, cowboy. But those things are pissed, and looking to you for direction. Doesn't your Book say that Lucifer betrayed God, and took a third of the angels with him?"

Dan shook his head, and blood spattered the ground. "I don't think it's in the book, exactly, but that's the story."

Mendelson sighed. "My crowd doesn't have a Lucifer, did you know that?" Dan shook his head. The Fed continued, "Oh, there's a Satan, but he's not your devil with horns and all; he's just the adversary, the challenger. He sort of wanders around, pointing out men's faults to God."

"Satan's a tattle-tale?"

Mendelson nodded. "More or less. But yours is the ultimate baddy."

"With what's going on around here, I'm more inclined to go with our version."

"But what if it's somewhere in between, cowboy? What if you are some kind of antichrist—in the strictest sense? A Jesus mock-up?"

Dan shuddered. "What if I didn't know who my father was?"

Mendelson just looked at him.

"What if I got tired of telling on men, and decided to walk in their shoes for a bit? What if I got tossed out of heaven, but ditched my buddies? Are they who I betrayed? Which story is it, Mendelson?"

A nearby explosion rocked both men out of their discussion. They turned and saw the hospital burning. Soldiers were firing flames and grenades into the blaze, but a hundred smoldering corpses kept advancing.

Blood poured off of Dan's face. He sighed. "Either way, I guess it's show time."

"Hey, cowboy."

Dan turned. "Yeah?"

"If I'm right, could you maybe not tell the Big Guy about some of my filthier habits?"

The sheriff grinned at him and shook his hand. "Done."

Dan walked to the rubble that had been the hospital. He walked past the soldiers, waving them back. They retreated gladly. The creature that had first woken led the rest through the ashes toward Dan. Bodies of men, women and children slithered around each other, their flesh intermingling and separating again. Their eyes burned.

Dan stopped about thirty feet from them, holding his hands out, palms first. Blood flowed freely from his hands, dripping onto the ground. The lead creature spoke. "Do you recognize us?"

Dan nodded. "I do."

"We followed you, and you left us."

"Yes, I left you until the time was right. I had much to do first." The thoughts of his conversation with Mendelson swirled around in Dan's head as he tried to come up with the right answers for an exam given in a language he only half-understood. He meshed the mythos together, taking the best parts and mixing them with pure bullshit.

"And is the time right now?"

"Almost, but I need to ask you to follow me again. Will you?"

"We will."

Visions of a glittering, shimmering army of one hundred million angels swam in Dan's head. He saw himself, alone, wandering, wanting companionship yet not daring to approach a human being. He saw himself in a court of sorts, with a faceless judge, haranguing a pockmarked man. He saw himself, old, sitting in a café in Paris, with another old man, discussing good and evil. He stood in a desert, offering a man bread, a man he loved.

"Come then," he said, and he walked to the center of the fire. The angels followed him, the others approaching from over the hill, from the school. He waited until they were close; they pressed around him, close enough to touch him, but they hung back just a bit. He reached into the ground then, and his arms grew long. He reached through the ground until he found what he sought, a gas line, and he drew it back to him.

As the gas line breached the surface of the smoldering earth, he ruptured it, and the explosion knocked the watching soldiers onto their collective asses. Mendelson gasped as he caught a glimpse of hell, not a figurative place, but all too real.

And Dan led his angels into it.

**

Three weeks after the fire that destroyed the hospital in Bethel, Deputy Alex Wilson was driving his patrol car toward Johnson's gas station when he saw a man walking along the road, alone. He wasn't going to stop, afraid that any complication would delay his date with Sheena, but then his conscience pricked him, and he slowed down, pulling up next to the man.

"You okay, buddy?" he asked, then he gasped. The man was nearly invisible, a melted CDC suit clinging tightly to his ash-caked form, but the light of a street lamp behind him shone through him. "Dan?"

"Just one thing, Deputy," said Dan before he vanished. "If anybody ever starts a religion after me, I will come back and kick the ever-living shit out of you."

Zakku Al Rada: Aftermath

The rain fell in waves, pattering against the roof of Shannon's makeshift shelter. She had cobbled it together from the ruins of the Republic's New Gideon administrative center. The rain was black and laden with ashes.

Shannon's uniform was in tatters, and she suffered from several minor burns where her flesh had been exposed. Only luck had spared her life. She had been inside the center's reinforced war room doing a routine systems check when the destruction had come. Her luck hadn't held though. In the two days since the firestorm swept across the world of New Gideon, she'd encountered no other survivors. She found herself slowly starving to death as she wandered the ruins of the city, never daring to go too far from where she had established her makeshift camp.

She picked at her nails, nervously raking her mind again for an explanation of what had happened. Shannon cursed herself for not paying more attention in the courses that she had been assigned before becoming an officer on this damn planet. One of the courses she had been required to take had dealt with communications technology. Maybe if she hadn't been so smug, she might have stood a chance of modifying some of the surviving equipment into a beacon, or something equally useful. But none of that mattered now. The past was the past, and the present was where she was trapped.

Finally, exhaustion overcame her, and she made a pillow of her jacket on the muddy ground beneath the wobbly steel roof of her shelter. She stretched out on the still warm ground and rolled up her sleeve, injecting herself with a sedative from her severely limited cache of supplies. Her dreams were strange and terrible since the firestorm, haunted by images of the burnt and torn bodies of her friends and by creatures unlike anything she'd ever seen.

In this *new* dream, Shannon stood at the edge of a forest too beautiful for words. She watched the crystalline leaves of the trees sparkle and dance on the gentle breeze under the star-filled sky. Even in her dream, she knew this wasn't right. Where were the nightmares that had plagued her? How could she dream of something so wonderful with so many dead around her?

"Shannon Burke," a voice called. She whirled around, scanning the landscape for its source. It was only then that she realized the voice had come from her very thoughts.

"Who . . . What are you?" she asked aloud.

"We did not mean to cause such suffering," the voice answered. "Come to us, Shannon Burke, and we will stop your pain."

"Come to you?" Shannon muttered, lost in confusion. "Where?"

"Zakku Al Rada lies west of the city. You can make the journey in three days on foot if you hurry."

"What are you?" Shannon asked again, wondering if she was losing her mind.

"We are your friends, Shannon," the voice purred.

Shannon awoke, sitting up so quickly that she nearly bumped her head against her shelter's low roof. She wrapped her arms about herself and shivered as the warm rain blew in to caress her. She crawled out into the rain and got to her feet. Looking up at New Gideon's nearest sun, she gauged the direction in which she would need to travel and then set out, heading west.

Things got even stranger as she chased after the phantasm of her dreams. Each day during her travels, she awoke someplace other than where she had slept, as if she kept walking through the real world in her dreams. She had heard of such things in old Earth myth but never once imagined that such a thing could actually happen.

On the third morning, Shannon awoke at the edge of the forest from her dreams. Around her were the twisted and burnt remains of four Alliance rovers. She nearly screamed at the sight of the man who sat watching her. He was more bone than flesh, with bits of metal cooked into his form. On the scraps of skin remaining, thousands of burns oozed yellow pus. The sockets of his eyes were empty black spaces, and yet she felt his gaze burrowing into her.

"Shannon," he whispered, extending a hand to help her to her feet. She slapped it away and covered her mouth, trying desperately to overcome dry heaves.

"I'm human, Shannon, like you. You have nothing to fear from me."

"You're dead," Shannon shot back.

"There's more than one way to be alive," the man laughed. "My friends have given me new life."

"Some friends," Shannon remarked, barely forcing herself to stay.

"My name is Dr. Sedric Ah-Val. Do you remember me?"

Shannon shook her head.

"I came to this world a few weeks ago with an expedition sponsored by the Alliance government. I passed through your city with my group on my way to this forest. The Alliance sent me to contact an alien race which dwells inside those trees," the man pointed at the woods. "I am happy to say that I was able to reach them, Shannon, but our intrusion here forced them to take action against us."

"The firestorm," Shannon breathed.

"Yes, they had to punish us for our sins on their world." The man rose to his feet. "And now, they have realized that it won't be enough. Humanity's greed and evil must be kept from spreading even farther through the stars. But they cannot leave this forest. So you and I, Shannon, we must help them. Through our bodies, they shall create a new breed of Fey like themselves to live amid the stars and keep humankind in check."

Shannon watched the black holes of his eyes. Even in their darkness, she could see madness raging inside him. She grabbed a rock as he moved towards her, and she lashed out, striking him square in what was left of his face.

He staggered backwards as Shannon rolled to her feet and took off running.

She'd only made it a few yards before her body froze. She stood still like a statue, although she fought to move with all her will.

The skeleton that had once been Ah-Val walked slowly to her. His eyes ran up and down her body. "Yes, Shannon, we shall help them. You'll see. You will be mother of a new race and will live in their songs forever."

Shannon screamed inside her mind as she felt his bone fingers touch her cheek.

"Who knows, Shannon? It might even be fun for both of us." The thing laughed as it lowered her to the ground and began to remove her clothes.

Coughing Fits

Jacob listened to the claws raking against the outer side of his apartment's wooden door, the slow taunting of a beast that knows its prey has no hope. Jacob glanced at his wristwatch. He still had a terrible flu and wanted this over as soon as possible so he could go back to his real pad and crash. He got to his feet and drew two old-fashioned .36 revolvers from the holsters under his arms. They were by no means the antiques they appeared to be. Each had been modified and had the firepower of a Magnum.

The apartment door exploded inward in a shower of splinters as the "wolf" came bounding inside. It stood over seven feet tall, thick layers of muscle rippled under its fur as it moved toward him. Jacob turned calmly to meet it and smiled as he fired both of his guns point blank into it. The rounds tore into its chest and knocked it from its feet. It hit the floor, wailing like a wounded dog.

"What took you so long?" Jacob muttered, his thumbs flipping back the hammers on both revolvers once more.

The wolf thing struggled to crawl away.

"I've got to do it," Jacob whispered to the wounded creature. "Besides, tardiness really pisses me off. You should have found me hours ago if you're half the killer I was told you are."

Jacob lowered the barrel of one of the revolvers to the creature's head and pulled the trigger. Red pulp and brain matter splattered across the floor of the apartment. Jacob sighed and tucked his guns away. He pulled a small headset from the pocket of his coat and slipped it on.

"Christy, send in the clean-up crew," he ordered. Then he bent over, coughing violently, almost collapsing to his knees. When the fit passed, he added over the com-link,

"And get me some more damn cough meds. I feel like shit up here."

Minutes later, a trio of black vans made their way across the Brooklyn Bridge. Jacob sat in the back of the lead van across from Christy, looking pale and tired. He gulped from a freshly opened bottle of cough syrup like it was a cold beer. He looked over at Christy. Her long blonde hair was pulled into a tight ponytail. Her laptop was open in front of her on her knees. Jacob burst into coughing again.

"You really should get Doc to take a look at you," she suggested with pity in her voice.

"Jeez," Jacob cursed, "I got the job done didn't I? A lot of people still work when they're sick."

"A lot of people don't even believe in things that go bump in the night, Jacob. *You* kill them. It's not a job that you should do at anything less than top form unless you want to end up dead. Look, we don't have anything else to deal with tonight. How about you go home and get some rest?"

Jacob grinned at her. "You read my mind. Sure, go ahead and pay off Doc and the crew and send 'em back to base."

"Ok, but what about us then?"

"We're going to stay right here, check into a local hotel, get some rest, and wait."

"But I thought you wanted to go home?"

"I do, but the job's not over," Jacob informed her.

"The wolf's dead, Jay. How much more over can it get?" Christy asked.

"It's not alone here, Christy. It can't be the one we were sent to kill. It went down too easy."

"What?" Christy blurted out in shock. "My God, then why are we sending the team home? We can't face them alone!"

"Look, truth is, I am dying. This isn't some simple cold or flu. It's cancer, alright? I don't want to die in bed, and the wolves have to be dealt with tonight before they decide to run or go underground. I'm not asking you to stay. I just figured there was no way in hell you would leave, no matter what I did or said."

Christy smiled.

The other two vans of Jacob's team turned and headed for the airport as Jacob's van drove onward into the seedier part of the city. He had taken the wheel himself and dismissed the agent who had been driving. He and Christy found a sinkhole of a motel and got a room. He tipped the owner over five grand, figuring the man would need it for repairs in the aftermath of what Jacob had in mind for tonight.

Christy followed Jacob upstairs to their third floor room and lingered outside the door. She was never great with goodbyes, but she knew Jacob may have let her stay in the city but he would never let her face what was actually coming with him.

"So this it then?" she asked.

"I hope so," Jacob answered watching tears well up in her eyes. "I've signed all the papers I had you draw up on the way here. All my accounts should be in your name by tomorrow morning. Just make sure you and Doc don't screw up my business, okay?"

Christy tried to smile but found that she couldn't. She turned and walked down the stairs without looking back. "I'll miss you," he heard her say under her breath. Jacob watched her go and then opened the door and went inside.

The room was much cleaner than he had hoped. A roach skittered across the floor beneath his feet, and he laughed until another coughing fit hit him so hard that he was forced to sit down on the edge of the room's single bed. His throat felt as if he had swallowed a handful of razor blades, his lungs heavy inside his chest. He lay back on the bed and closed his eyes.

They would find him soon enough.

Around 3 A.M., someone or something knocked on the door. He awoke with a start, his eyes watering, but he managed not to cough. He knew if he started he might not be able to stop this time. He picked up a bottle of cough medicine from the nightstand and took a slug of it.

"Jacob Morris?" a thick, cold voice called from the hallway. "Jacob, are you in there?"

Jacob didn't answer. He jerked his revolvers into his hands and fired through the door. The thing outside screamed as the silver bullets burst through the thin wood and into its belly. In a blur of movement, almost too fast for the human eye, a wolf leapt through the room's window and landed on its feet in the center of the room as three others ripped the door from its hinges and poured inside.

Jacob spun in a half circle, firing as he moved. His guns thundered four times, wounding three of the creatures, but the largest beast dodged the round he'd meant for it with ease. The movement taxed Jacob's tired body beyond its limits, and he began to cough, hacking up mouthfuls of blood.

The largest of the creatures moved towards Jacob. The others thrashed and howled, bleeding to death on the floor as the silver in their bloodstreams poisoned them. The uninjured wolf grabbed Jacob by his neck and lifted him effortlessly into the air. He could feel its fingers digging into the flesh of his neck, could feel warm liquid dribbling down the sides of his throat. The wolf-thing looked Jacob in the eyes, and he saw that it understood. It wanted vengeance on the one who had killed its pack mate, and Jacob wanted death with dignity just as it would.

In one fluid motion, it tore Jacob's head free from his body and tossed it across the room, then whirled, leaping out the third floor window into the night, into the street below. It disappeared into the shadows long before the squealing police sirens arose in the distance.

The Price of Arrogance

Red emergency lights flickered throughout the station's corridors as Aleks ran for the bridge. His breath, coming in ragged gasps, fogged the faceplate of his bio-suit. The unthinkable had happened, and there was little hope of survival beyond the next few hours.

The ZX virus had gotten loose. He didn't know how and could only pray he donned his bio-suit in time to escape infection. At that exact moment, he knew an Alliance war cruiser was being dispatched to eradicate the station and all its inhabitants to prevent the spread of the ZX virus into Alliance space; however, the warship was the least of his worries. He had much more immediate concerns to deal with.

The ZX virus was the ultimate achievement in bio-warfare. It was an airborne virus which not only spread like wildfire but was both fatal in the long term and caused acute homicidal rage until the virus eventually burned out the host's body. The virus attached itself to a host's neural system, causing an intense state of pain and madness, and now, Aleks was perhaps the only living soul on the station not infected.

Reaching the entrance to the station's bridge, Aleks frantically typed his access codes into the locking panel on the door. He failed twice before he was able to steady his trembling hands enough to enter the codes. The huge blast doors of the bridge finally dilated, but he found the bridge empty of other survivors. It was obvious, however, that someone had been here. The bridge looked like a war zone. Several small electrical fires raged amid the broken consoles and there were bloodstains all over the walls and floor. Aleks rushed onto the bridge and locked the blast doors behind him.

He headed straight for the communications terminal. It was destroyed beyond his ability to repair it. He was a doctor not an engineer. Aleks checked the station's power core readings from another terminal that was still somewhat functional. It appeared the station's failsafe self-destruct mechanism hadn't been activated. He quickly accessed its system and typed in the proper codes to prevent it from activating itself, then sat down in the command chair. Tears ran down his already sweat-drenched cheeks as he wondered what in the hell he was going to do now. He thought of the escape pods but instantly discarded that idea. He didn't want to gamble encountering infected members of the crew in their current state. Besides, there were no habitable planets the pods could reach before their life support systems expired.

Aleks jumped as something or someone slammed against the outer side of the bridge's blast doors. He rushed over to the security console as whatever it was struck the doors a second time, sending a loud boom reverberating throughout the bridge. On the console's monitor, he saw Lieutenant Burke standing outside the doors to the bridge, staring up at the security camera. The man was smiling though his left arm dangled limply at his side, obviously dislocated and fractured from his assault on the blast doors. Then, for no apparent reason, Burke threw his head back, screamed at the top of his lungs and hurled himself at the doors. Aleks could hear bone crunching against metal.

Aleks flipped off the monitor. He couldn't take looking at Burke anymore. He sank back into the command chair and knew what had to be done. There wasn't going to be any escape for him. He had sealed his fate when he had signed on to be a part of the research team here, developing the virus. He flipped open the access to the self-destruct device again and withdrew the codes he had entered. He watched as the device came to life as its timer began to tick down the thirty seconds that he'd set. Aleks closed his eyes and waited.

The research station lit up the stars as its power core overloaded, and it sparkled in the void like a fireworks display as explosions ripped through every inch of its mass.

Icy Roads

"The Dead Walk": this headline was all people talked about since the first paper to bear it had hit the stands a few weeks back, though no one really knew what to say. It was a Tuesday in the small North Carolina town where Jennifer worked and lived, and she had other problems. Foremost on her mind was the weather. She needed to be at the store by 7 AM to do her morning paperwork. She'd only recently been promoted to manager and always worried about having the paperwork to her boss at the regional office on time. She crawled out of bed and made her way downstairs, flicking on the radio as she grabbed some cold pop-tarts for breakfast.

School closings were the top news of the morning. Only one school over in Boone somewhere had been closed because of the dead plague, the rest because of the heavy white flakes that poured from the heavens outside her window. Jennifer was deathly afraid of driving in bad weather and sat down at the kitchen table, staring at the mess outside. She sipped cold coffee left over from last night and wondered if she should even try to make it in or call someone else who lived closer. She had a great staff and knew Lois could handle it if she didn't show, yet she felt she had to be there. She stood up and got her coat off the back of the chair and shrugged it onto her shoulders, heading outside into the storm. The morning air stung her exposed flesh as she raced over to her car and fired it up. She headed back into the house to get ready while the car's heater worked on the layer of ice over its windshield.

A few minutes later, with a cigarette dangling between her lips, Jennifer slid into to the now warm car and carefully backed down her drive. The car slipped a bit at the end of the drive as it lurched onto the main road, but she kept it under control. Setting out at a painfully slow crawl, she drove towards town. Fear of wrecking was the only thing that kept her foot off the accelerator. As she sat at the stop sign near the main interstate between her home and the store, she noticed a man walking towards her car through the snow. At first she felt sorry for the poor man and thought of offering him a ride into town. But as he drew nearer, she realized there was something strange about the way he was walking. As he lumbered underneath the glow of the streetlights, she got a clear look at him. Blood caked the edges of his lips, and his face was pale, encrusted with ice. His eyes were rolled back in his head, showing only white. The three-piece suit he wore was covered in mud and something red.

Quickly, Jennifer hit the lock button, sealing the car as the man shuffled closer. She looked around, frantically searching for someone else, but the interstate was quiet and there was no sign of any other car anywhere. *Oh God*, she thought. *Is he dead?* She had never seen one of the dead up close, only in the papers and on TV. She felt her heart pounding in her chest, threatening to burst. Jennifer floored the pedal and roared out onto the road. She watched the figure growing smaller in her rearview and shuddered. She'd been lucky that there had been only one of them and that she had been in the car.

Suddenly, she hit a patch of ice and veered left. The car spun out of control as she screamed, dropping her cigarette to the floorboard. She wrestled with the wheel, straining to regain control as the car went off the road. Jennifer was flung forward in her seat as the car smashed into a tree, and the engine went dead to the sickening crunch of bone and metal. Through blurred vision, Jennifer looked out at the flattened hood; tears welled up in her eyes. Her right leg felt like hell, and blood was leaking through her dress pants where the white of her bone protruded. Jennifer wrenched open her door and leaned out, vomiting onto the road's shoulder. Her hand found the seatbelt release, and she tumbled out of the car onto the pavement, yelling; her leg felt as if it were being torn off. Jennifer fought not to black out and started screaming for help. Remembering the flares in her trunk, she started to drag her body towards the back of the car.

She saw him again then, the dead man still working his way down the road towards her. Panic ripped through her veins. She jerked herself to her feet, using the car to pull herself up, and watched him grow ever closer. She felt the bile rising in her throat again, but had no time to be sick. She abandoned the flares and the car and took off, limping down the road away from the man. There was a rest area not too far ahead. Surely someone would be there.

Jennifer made it a few steps before a second figure came bounding out of the trees ahead of her. This one was a woman, young like herself and so freshly dead that red liquid still poured and steamed from the chewed-out holes of her throat. Jennifer tried to shove the woman away as she grabbed at her face. Two long nails managed to slash Jennifer's cheek all the same.

Jennifer twisted her leg, howling as she fell to the ground. The woman threw herself onto Jennifer, ripping and biting at her. The woman's teeth sunk into Jennifer's shoulder as the man finally arrived. The last thing Jennifer saw as her world went black was his maw of yellow teeth dropping towards her throat.

Indigs

"Nobody ever told me that it was going to be like this," Greg said as he steered the tank into the remnants of the village.

Harrison laughed over the tank's internal com-system "What did you expect, Kid?" Harrison was the tank's gunner and a long-time veteran of missions such as this one. "We sweep through and clean out the natives so the colonization fleet doesn't have any problems when it arrives. It's a good job, not much of a chance of getting your ass shot off on a world like this."

Greg drove through a hut of mud and wood, the treads of the tank grinding bodies into the soil.

"It just doesn't seem right," Greg said. "These people don't have any way of even trying to fight back."

"The day I start feeling sorry for a bunch of blue-skinned primitives, Kid, is the day I resign my commission. Remember, we're doing this for Earth and the Alliance. Just like Rome, the Alliance will die if it ever stops expanding. Worlds like this are easy to take and we need them."

To the tank's left, something moved among the burnt rubble of the village. Greg started to shout a warning, but Harrison was already bringing the tank's anti-personnel guns to bear on the position.

Wearing only loose animal hides about his lower body, a blue-skinned native hopped up from his hiding place. Long silver hair spilled over his naked shoulders as he raised a spear against the hulking metal monster. Harrison fired a quick, single burst, nearly vaporizing the man's torso. Greg imagined the smile on the veteran's face as Harrison shouted, "See! Easy, Kid! Easy!"

Greg looked out his view port, taking in the destruction surrounding them. "I don't know," Greg said. "I think I'd rather be facing someone who could at least shoot back."

In the gunner's compartment, Harrison frowned while scanning the village for more targets.

***

From the cover of the trees, Amrin watched the monster demolish his people. Sweat glistened on his light-green skin as the hot blood of anger boiled inside his veins. Standing behind him, Amelian placed a hand onto his shoulder. "Now is not the time," she said quietly.

Amrin whirled around, slapping her hand away. "When will the time come, priestess?" he spat. He glanced around at his warriors. They stood tall and proud, unafraid of the monster that now sat motionless in the center of the village. "We are ready to die if need be. Tell us how to stop that thing, and it shall not kill again."

Amelian felt her heart crumble inside her chest as he continued to rage.

"You are the voice of God, priestess! Surely, he has told you how to slay the beast. It cannot be his will that we all perish while the pink skins and their monsters take our world from us. Tell us, priestess, and let us carry out God's will."

Amelian looked away from the war chief, turning her eyes downward towards the ground.

"There is a way," she said in no more than a whisper, "but it is not permitted."

Amrin snarled, grabbing the front of Amelian's black robes and pulling her to him. He jerked her face up towards his own. "We are dying, Amelian. All of us." He released her so quickly that she staggered a step backwards. "If there is a way, you must tell us before it is too late."

Everyone that was gathered in the forest waited for her to speak. The masses of women and children that were huddled among the ranks of Amrin's men watched her with expectant faces.

Tears formed in Amelian's eyes, running down her cheeks. "We are not ready for the way," she said finally.

Amrin struck her, a sharp backhanded blow that knocked her from her feet. He squatted beside her sprawling form, drawing his knife. The blade was speckled with the dried red flakes of pink-skin blood. He leaned over her, pressing the blade's point against her throat. "I am sorry, Amelian, but I don't have time to become enlightened enough for your liking. I need to know now. I will not stand by and watch our race fade into the eternal night."

"The stones!" Amelian cried. "The stones are our only hope!"

Amrin withdrew the knife, a look of confusion and shock upon his face. *"What?"*

Amelian rubbed at her throat. "Yes, the stones."

Amrin rocked with laughter, a deep madness in his eyes. "The stones bring the rains and keep the desert from our valley. Do you plan to *drown* the beasts, perhaps blast them with sand?"

"No," Amelian answered, getting to her feet. "The stones are much more. They were left behind when God departed from this world. They were the tools he used during the shaping." She waved her arm around, gesturing towards the trees. "They created all that we have, but they can be used for unmaking things as well. They hold the power of the stars inside them."

Amrin grinned. "Then lead me to them, priestess."

Amelian loosened her robes and let them drop from her body. Imbedded in her skin between the mounds of her breasts, a gem of deep purple seemed to pulsate along with her heart. "Each of the eighteen members of my order carries one, one for each of our villages. When we pass on, it is cut from our flesh and given to our chosen successor. It is a part of the Almighty and is alive inside our bodies." Amelian's fingers stroked its surface. Energy from within the gem leapt to meet her fingertips, crackling in its intensity. "You have but to slay me, Amrin, and it will be yours."

"Forgive me," Amrin whispered as he slid his blade into her belly. Warm, green blood rushed out over his hand.

"I do," Amelian said as he twisted the knife, cutting upwards towards her heart and the gem.

The forest was silent as Amrin hacked away the flesh surrounding the gem.

***

Harrison slammed his fist into the gunnery controls, frustrated and disgusted by the lack of targets. The sensors had swept the village a dozen times to reveal nothing more.

"Sarge, it looks like our job here is done," Greg said. "Alpha platoon is requesting support for their raid on the village to the north. Are you ready to move out?"

"I know somebody's still here." Harrison grunted. "I can feel it, but the sensor sweeps keep coming up clean."

Suddenly, Harrison's screen surged with an energy reading so powerful that it overloaded the array. The screen went dead. "Damn!" Harrison yelled, already trying to switch to the back-up circuits.

"What the hell was that?" Greg's voice shouted over the intercom.

"Don't know," Harrison mumbled as the sensors came online again. The screen was full of life signatures, over three dozen spilling out of the distant tree line and closing on the tank's position.

Blue-skinned warriors ran across the open field between the forest and the village, waving weapons made of bone and wood. The lead warrior didn't read as a normal blip on the screen. Instead, the limited AI recognized him as a tank with an energy readout greater than the fusion drive of *Harrison's* tank.

Harrison maneuvered the turret towards the new targets as Greg revved the tank into motion and sped towards the warriors. Harrison smirked as he brought the main gun into action. The tank shook as it fired. The field exploded into a blaze of fire and light. Greg could hear the screams of the dying natives over the roar of the tank's engine. Before the initial blast had faded, Harrison started sweeping the area with the anti-personnel guns. They chattered, spitting death into the sea of flame and smoke.

A lone man, bleeding and battered, still stood, surrounded by the twisted and smoking forms of his companions.

"Oh, God," Greg muttered, feeling pity for the man.

Harrison sighted the anti-personnel guns onto their remaining target. "That bastard's going down this time!"

The man wobbled and nearly fell, but somehow, despite his gaping wounds, remained on his feet. He outstretched a hand towards the tank. Harrison hesitated, his finger on the trigger, "What's that F-er doing?"

A bolt of purple energy shot from the man's fingertips, slicing through the air. It struck the tank's armor and melted through it, striking the tank's fuel cell. The entire village lit up as the tank exploded.

***

As his purple energy receded, Amrin fell to his knees. Women, children, and the few warriors left emerged from the trees and ran towards him. Their triumphant cries rang in the air. When they reached Amrin, they saw that he was dead, his body an empty and withered shell. One of the warriors pushed Amrin's corpse to the ground and began sawing at the flesh surrounding the gem imbedded in Amrin's chest. The warrior tore his prize free and held it high into the sun's rays. "Now, we have a way to fight!" he screamed, shaking the gem at the heavens. Applause and cheers sounded all around him.

Hungry

Lucas lay in the ditch, staring with disbelief at the metal spike that pierced his lower leg. The pain was almost unbearable, but at least he had managed to stop screaming. Sweat glistened on his skin despite the cold of the night. He knew he had to do something. They were coming, of that he had no doubt. They didn't seem to have ears, but he knew they heard him all the same. He looked around for his 9mm and saw it laying a few feet out of reach. He'd dropped it when he'd stumbled into the ditch.

He heard them running through the brush of the woods towards him. He jerked his body in the direction of the gun. His fingers closed about its grip as the spike twisted and tore free of his flesh. He howled and nearly blacked out as the big one's face popped over the side of the ditch. He looked up into its gleaming red eyes and its purple, slick, smooth skin. The sphincter of its mouth dilated, revealing rows of razor teeth that seemed to stretch all the way down its throat as it hissed at him.

Lucas lifted the pistol and put a shot between its eyes. Shrieking, it either pulled or fell away from the edge of the ditch. He doubted very much that the thing was dead. When Lucas had been forced to bail out he'd had no idea he'd be parachuting into hell nor did he have any idea what the fuck these things were, but he knew one thing for sure: they weren't natural to the earth. At least, not any part of the earth he knew. He wondered if they were the reason that the Russians had set up a "no fly" zone over the area, the reason his plane had been shot down. Maybe they were some kind of "Red" experiment in biological warfare, but if so, they were a masterpiece, strong, fast, and deadly.

A gargled hiss echoed in the night as the one he'd shot leaned back over the edge of the ditch, grinning at him.

Then suddenly, three more leapt down around him where he lay. They carried primitive spears and rusted saw blades in their misshapen, four-fingered hands.

Lucas cracked off three shots into the closest one's chest, sending it reeling backwards, leaking black pus. The others attacked. He felt the stone tip of the second one's spear punch through his sternum as he looked into the third's hungry eyes which hovered above the drooling orifice of its face.

With the last of his strength, Lucas shoved his 9mm into his own mouth and pulled the trigger. The bullet exited the back of his skull, spraying the snow-covered grass with brain-matter.

The creatures hissed and danced about his corpse. Tonight, they would be eating American food for the first time.

Family

RJ sat in the passenger seat, grinning like the devil. He cradled an AK-47 in his lap. Leper had asked him several times where he'd gotten the rifle, but RJ wasn't talking.

Leper sat in the back of the car with Drake, who still looked pissed because he wasn't riding shotgun on this little venture. Drake had his window rolled down, but the inside of the car still boiled with second hand smoke from the countless cigarettes he'd smoked already. He tossed another butt out of the car and instantly lit up again.

Hal didn't mind being the driver. Somehow, it made him feel like there was less blood on his hands. He took the exit ramp down Bleaker Street and guided the vehicle towards Charleston drive.

"You think they'll really be there?" Leper asked, leaning up between Hal and RJ. His breath stunk like a decaying corpse. "I sure as Hell wouldn't be if I was them!"

"Shut the fuck up!" RJ snapped, shoving Leper back onto his seat.

"He has a point, RJ," Hal said without taking his eyes off the road.

"They'll be there," Drake answered around the cigarette, slipping his own 9mm from his jacket pocket and checking the clip. "They always are."

Hal rounded the corner of Bleaker and Charleston, and sure enough, they were. Martin and his cronies were sprawled out on the steps of their apartment building, smoking and yapping it up. Martin noticed their car as soon as it came into view. He started shouting and tried to pull his friends to their feet. RJ leaned out the window and let loose on full-auto.

Ears hurting as the weapon barked and spat death, Hal watched as Martin caught the brunt of RJ's first burst dead on, watched as Martin's body twitched and leapt and fell to the ground. Drake dropped his cigarette onto the floorboards, popping off a few rounds with his 9mm as Hal stomped on the accelerator.

In the rearview, Hal could see the bodies laying on the pavement in growing pools of red as he sped away. It didn't look like any of them had been lucky enough to get away in time.

"Shit, man!" RJ howled with joy, slapping the dashboard so hard that it cracked. Drake and Leper were shouting, too. Hal whirled the car down an alley and cut across to another road, which led away from the scene behind them.

"We fuckin' *smoked* those bastards!" RJ laughed.

"Hey, Drake. . ." Hal said.

"What man?" Drake answered still high on bloodlust and adrenaline.

"Would you mind getting your cigarette the hell off my floor?"

Everyone fell silent.

Drake blinked. "Shit, man, sorry." Drake picked up the butt and tossed it out the window. He wet his fingers with spit and tried to wipe at the burnt place in the floor mat.

Eventually, RJ turned to glance at Hal. "What ya doin' later tonight, man? Ya wanna catch that new fuck flick over at Joe's?"

Hal shook his head. "Naw, I'll pass."

"Hal don't need no flick, man, he's gettin' enough from Sarah!" Leper whooped.

Drake laughed, but RJ whirled on them. "Leave the fucker alone! You freaks ever even seen a pussy?"

No one in the back answered.

"Look, I gotta get goin'," Hal said. "Where should I drop you guys at?"

"Right here will be fine," RJ ordered as Hal drove by Riker's Pub. Hal pulled up to the curb and stopped the car, leaving the engine running. Drake and Leper hopped out, but RJ lingered in his seat, tucking his rifle inside the depths of his long coat. "You okay, Hal?"

"Yeah, sure man. Fine."

RJ nodded and got out, slamming the door behind him. He leaned back into the car through the open passenger window. "You'll catch up with us later, right?"

"Yeah, man, if I can."

Hal pulled back out onto the road. With the others gone, he flipped on the radio. Hot tears burned in his eyes. He'd had enough of this shit. Maybe he was just too old for it now, or maybe he was just becoming human again. He knew RJ would kill him if he tried to leave so he'd planned everything so carefully. Sarah would be waiting for him with their bags ready. They'd leave the city tonight before RJ even realized they were gone. Hal hummed with the music as he drove on towards the new life he'd share with Sarah.

Hal parked his car across the street from their home and walked up the steps. There was still a bit of daylight spilling over the tops of the buildings around him. He wondered if Sarah would be ready yet. As he climbed the steps to the door of the building, he heard a voice from behind him.

"Goin' somewhere, Hal?"

Hal whirled around to see RJ and his friends standing on the street below the steps. RJ's coat bulged with the AK-47. Drake and Leper had the "look" in their eyes. They were expecting blood.

"What's it to you?" Hal shot back, knowing he shouldn't have.

"You're mine, Hal!" RJ roared. "You're a member of this family, and you have responsibilities to us! I am not going to let you go running off with that little whore!"

Hal had no weapon. His eyes darted around, seeking anything he could use to defend himself with. No luck. He turned and ran for the building's door.

Leper giggled as he drew the .38 from his pants pocket and nailed Hal right between the shoulders. RJ hit Leper so hard the little guy fell over onto the street, spitting teeth. "You little shit. That's Hal you just shot. He may be fucked up, but he's still family!"

"Sorry," Leper tried to say as blood poured from his mouth.

Hal lay on the steps, still trying to crawl towards the door. RJ walked over to him and placed a foot on Hal's back. Hal screamed at the pain of RJ pressing down on his wound. "Hal, Hal, Hal, what am I going to do with you?"

At that moment, the door opened and Sarah stepped out into the glow of the streetlights. Leper and Drake burst into laughter from the darkness below as she saw RJ standing over Hal's crumpled form. RJ looked up at her. "Go away, Sarah; this is family business."

Without answering, she leapt at RJ, her fingernails streaking towards his face. RJ tried to dodge, but the thunder of a 9mm made him curve his attempt so that he went down on his knees. The bullet struck Sarah in the throat, and she fell over him, making a horrible gargling sound. RJ shoved aside her bleeding corpse and jumped up, wiping at the red stain on his coat.

"Jesus," he muttered, shooting a look at Drake. "Be a little more careful next time."

"There won't be a next time," a hollow, wheezing voice said as Sarah stood up. "Your time is over."

RJ stared at her in disbelief, his gaze lingering on the hole in her throat. She grabbed him, lifting him from his feet with a single hand. Drake and Leper watched in horror as she simply ripped him in two. RJ's intestines and organs spilt onto the steps as she discarded his lower half and waved his torso at the pair.

Drake and Leper turned, running into the darkness. Sarah's laughter echoed in the surrounding alleys. She leaned down beside Hal, who was now unconscious from blood loss. "I hadn't planned to take you so soon," she whispered, "but your friends have left me no choice. Don't worry; you'll have the new life you sought. It will be glorious and wondrous in ways you never imagined. And it shall be eternal!" She pressed her long fangs into his neck, and Hal's world changed forever.

From Heaven, Into Hell

It was both the best and worst day of Jeremiah's life. The good news was that he'd just made the find of a lifetime. There would be no more endless days spent breaking his back just to pan a few nuggets here and there out of Topher river. No more endless meals of dried beans and stale bread. The Lord had finally given him his due: a shooting star that had blazed its way through the clouds, brighter than the noonday sun. Sure it had blown the tarnation out of his old shack and made one hell of a hole to boot, but he didn't care because the orb looked like it weighed over thirty pounds, and it glimmered like gold. Jeremiah knew in his heart that it was the purest gold he'd ever seen.

The bad news was that he was now laying in the dirt, bleeding to death. After three grueling hours of carrying water from the river to cool the thing down, he'd noticed that old Lucas was riding up the mountain to his prospect. He knew Lucas must've seen the thing as it fell and was coming to see what it was. No matter how much money he owed the old bastard, he wasn't about to let Lucas take what was his. Jeremiah's rifle had been in his shack when the Lord had sent the rock from the heavens, though, and the gun had turned into a puddle of metal on the crater's right edge. Wasn't gonna do him no good in a shape like that. So he'd crouched down in the crater and prayed that Lucas would just go on by. Jeremiah had never been known for his quick thinking.

Lucas rode up to the edge and called out to him. *Shit*, Jeremiah thought and pulled his hunting knife. It was all he had, but he wasn't about to give up the Lord's gift without a fight. He yelled at the top of his lungs and ran up the slope towards Lucas. The old man stared at him in disbelief until it sunk in that Jeremiah meant business. He drew his .36 revolver and popped Jeremiah twice in the chest. Jeremiah toppled and rolled down into the crater to where he lay now, watching the old man make his way unsteadily down to the orb. The moment he had seen it, all thoughts of Jeremiah had fled his mind. The bastard was practically drooling over the gold.

Then, the unthinkable happened. The gold shattered, hatching like an egg. At first, Jeremiah thought the Lord had done it to prevent the orb from falling into the wrong hands. But then something started coming out of the crack. Jeremiah squinted his eyes to see better, and then his eyes widened. Tiny metal demons swarmed like fire ants across the dirt towards him. Each had eight legs and a single glowing dot where eyes should be.

Lucas's attention snapped back to Jeremiah as the man howled and crawled towards the edge of the pit, slapping at his own body with his hands. Lucas didn't know what to make of it, and he sure wasn't about to take chances with no crazy man. He raised his .36 and shot Jeremiah straight between the eyes. Jeremiah's body thrashed a second longer, then lay still. Lucas shrugged and picked up a piece of the broken orb, biting into to it with his teeth. A grin stretched across his face. He crammed the piece into his pocket and leaned over to fish up more.

"Lucas Martin of Sol Three," a voice boomed from behind him. He whirled around to see Jeremiah back on his feet, his eyes glowing a deep green. His shirt was stained red and a trickle of blood oozed from the hole in his forehead, but there he stood, plain as day.

"Jesus!" Lucas wailed. He emptied his colt's last round into Jeremiah's stomach, but the man didn't even flinch. He began to walk towards Lucas with his hands outstretched. "Lucas Martin of Sol Three," the thing croaked again in a hollow voice devoid of emotion.

Lucas didn't waste any more time. He ran as fast as could for his horse and hopped in the saddle, kicking the animal's flank with all his might. The beast grunted and took off, galloping away from the crater.

The thing that had been Jeremiah watched him flee, then turned its face towards the heavens. From its mouth erupted a chattering series of high-pitched clicks. *Contact has failed,* it informed the ship in orbit around the Earth. *The dominant species of Sol Three is too primitive at this stage of its development.* It cautioned against another attempt at contact for at least several more decades. It finished its communion with the others aboard the ship with one last sad clicking noise that echoed in the host body's throat.

Jeremiah's body erupted into blue flames and fell to the dust to burn away in nothingness beside the remnants of the golden orb.

Bad Mojo

I am so tired now. It is all I can do to hold my head up. My horse died of exhaustion two days ago. Since then, I have been running on foot. I can feel the one stalking me out there in the darkness, drawing closer.

I stare into the fire of my makeshift camp and watch the flames lick at the surrounding sand. The desert night is cold. Pulling my coat tighter about my body, I shiver and wait. It will be over soon. I can run no more.

There was a time when nothing frightened me, a time when my gun was faster, and that was enough. If only he were a man like me, I would face him down, but he is already dead. He is a legend.

That old squaw back in Dallas had conjured him up and had opened the very gates of Hell to unleash him. She will never forgive me for the deaths of her sons. They had it comin' though, that's for damn sure. Walkin' around the streets, flirtin' with the ladies like they were white men. Someone had to put them in their place. I have killed dozens of men in my life; how was I to know that killing two redskins would be my end? Had I known that the old squaw's magic was real, I would have shot her first.

I pick up a twig and poke at the fire, watching the glowing embers drift upwards on the breeze. In the edge of my vision, atop a nearby dune, something moves in the night. I hear his horse snort as I turn to look upon him.

He sits tall in the saddle, a grin upon his rotting face. He shall not stop until I am dead, and I have no hope for he is the Kid. There is no one faster.

Billy gets down from his horse, his bones creaking as he moves. His glowing blue eyes never leave me as he walks into camp and takes a seat across the fire from me. The night is silent. In the light of the blaze, I can see the worms wriggling and squirming around in his gray, putrid flesh. Then he speaks in a voice like heavy boots grinding gravel beneath their soles.

"Been huntin' for ya," he says. "About time we finished up, ain't it?"

I can only nod as I get to my feet and back away from his smell, a smell like spoiled meat left too long in the sun. There is no reasoning with the vengeful dead.

Billy gets up, too, the bones of his gun hand glistening in the starlight as his fingers twitch beside the holster on his belt. My own hand is trembling as I reach for my colt.

For a reason I can't explain, I open my mouth and the words come tumbling out: "I've always wanted to meet you, Billy. You were my hero."

He smiles and his leathery cheeks crack open from the movement, spilling maggots onto the sand.

I draw, but his hand is like a blur, his gun already thundering. The first bullet strikes my shoulder. I scream and watch my gun go bouncing away across the desert floor. His second shot blows out my right knee, and I fall into the sand.

He stands there for a moment, watching me bleed as I try to crawl toward my weapon. Pulling out a long knife from his belt, he laughs, dry heaving in a ruptured lung.

"Sorry, friend," he says, "but she said it had to be slow."

As he steps towards me, I close my eyes and wait for the feel of metal slicing into my scalp.

Fears

Lisa was getting ready to lock up for the night as a last car pulled into the video store's parking lot. Cursing under her breath, she left the doors open and headed back to the counter.

A lone man got out of the car. He was young, probably in his mid-twenties, and he wore black jeans and a matching jacket. Long dark hair spilled over his shoulders. He made his way inside and headed straight towards her. Without bothering to say hello, he asked, "Do you have any Fulci?"

Lisa's tired mind fought to make sense of the question as she stared into his blue eyes. "Excuse me?" she said.

"Fulci, the Italian director," the man said in an irritated tone.

"I don't think so," Lisa answered.

The man pulled a .38 revolver from his jacket pocket and pointed it at her face. Lisa blinked as her mouth went suddenly dry.

"That's too bad," the man purred. "I guess I'll just have to find another way to amuse myself tonight."

Lisa's heart thundered in her chest, and a slight layer of sweat began to form on her brow.

"Tell me," he asked leaning closer. "What are you afraid of?"

Lisa was so terrified that she told the truth. "The dumpsters. . . the dumpster out back. I can't stand to take the night trash out by myself. There's something inside of it. I don't know how, but it's always there, watching me, waiting for me to get too close."

"Really," the man grinned, feeding on her fear. "Show me."

"No!" Lisa squealed, "I can't. . . "

The man pulled back the revolver's hammer, clicking a round into place. He shoved the barrel against her forehead. "I said *show me*."

Lisa led him out back to the dumpsters, making sure to give them a wide berth. As the man examined them, something thumped inside the largest dumpster.

"Ah." He smiled, dragging a crate of trash over to its side. "Let's take a look at your fear."

The man climbed onto the crate and peered down into the dumpster. In a blur of movement almost too fast for the human eye, a large furry hand matted with blood and feces grabbed the front of his jacket and pulled him inside.

Lisa screamed as she heard the sickening snap of bones that echoed in the dumpster. She ran through the store's rear entrance, slamming the door behind her, and fell to her knees; tears burned in her eyes. The last thing Lisa heard before the blackness came was a beast-like roar as something tore the door from its hinges and entered the store.

A Game of Souls

Rolling an ace over withered fingers of dangling flesh and liver spots, Lucas thumps the card atop the shuffled deck. Below sunken eyes, his purple lips pull tight in the imitation of a grin. "Shall we play?"

Despite the sweat on his brow, Chad shivers. "It's been a long time, Lucas. Do we have to do this?"

"Fifty years ago, you were quite eager to play, my boy. Oh, you and I had a blast in New Orleans, didn't we? But that was then and this is now. There will be no welching. It's time for our second game."

Picking up the deck, Lucas begins to deal the cards. Each card thunders as he slaps it down on the table top in front Chad in the silence of the room.

"You didn't really expect me to let you get away with that one lucky hand did you? What you won is mine and I shall have it back."

Chad brushes his long black hair from his eyes, reaching into the pocket of his tattered leather jacket for his pack of Camels. With a trembling hand, he strikes his lighter and lights up. Chad reluctantly glances at the cards he has been dealt: a pair of three's, a five, a jack, a ten . . . it's not a bad hand. He knows it could have been worse.

"I'll make it easier on you Chad, if you fold."

"If I win, Lucas, you die, but what do I get in return for risking what I already have?"

"In fifty years of youth, I'm sure you dreamed up something to take your jadedness away."

Cards change, angels holding their breath to see where luck will lead. "Call," Lucas breathes.

Chad places his hand face down on the table but doesn't show them. He pauses for a moment, looking across the table at Lucas. Reaching under the table, Chad's fingers close around the hilt of the knife hidden in his boot. In one quick motion, he frees it from its sheath and swings at Lucas' neck. Lucas catches his arm. With a delicate twist, he cracks the bone, and Chad screams. Calmly, Lucas holds Chad's arm, and with his free hand, he begins to flip over the young man's cards.

"Let's see your hand. Ah, a pair of three's and nothing else. I'm afraid I have a straight flush, young man."

Chad's flesh wrinkles, hair falling out in handfuls as his spine bends with age. Standing from his chair straight and tall, Lucas looks down at the poor creature that Chad has become. Lucas inspects his own renewed form, his body healthy and young once more. "If you hadn't tried to welch, Chad, I would have killed you, as a mercy to one so old, but now, Chad, you shall live." Lucas walks out of the room, leaving Chad alone, clutching a broken arm to a skeletal chest. A tear slides down wrinkled flesh as Chad whimpers. The angels join him in his weeping as the devil leaves the building, laughing into the wind.

Between Two Worlds

The world of Greg's childhood was gone, a dimly remembered place of wonders lost and untold. Sometimes, if he tried very hard, he could recall something called a "Sunday drive"; his father would load him up into a thing that moved on wheels, and they would ride out to look at rows of houses on the wayside of the path. He could recall the touch of his mother as she pulled a blanket over him as he lay in bed at night. But now, they were dead, and he was no longer a child. He was twenty-two now, a man in a postwar world that had replaced the old one.

His horse snorted, protesting the fact that he was keeping it out in the rain. Greg held its reins in one hand and his .30-06 in the other. The downpour had long ago soaked through the layers of hides that he wore, and he shivered as the cold breeze cut through the trees of the surrounding woods. He had only two rounds for the rifle, and the town elders had risked much in trusting its use and care to him. Operating firearms for which ammunition could be found were almost as rare as gasoline in this new dark age of man. The elders had little choice, however, for in their eyes, only an old-world gun stood even a chance of stopping the beast, and its presence in these woods outside of town could no longer be overlooked. Only this morning, it had struck again, killing two children as they played outside the town's walls while the villagers had been harvesting the meager crops that the fall had brought.

New Hope was a small town of only seventy folk, all Christian and all trying to survive, yet it was the largest settlement for over a hundred miles. The war that ended the old world had left few alive and had left even fewer places safe enough to dwell in, free of fallout and mutants. Mutations arose everywhere in the years after the fall among the human and animal kingdoms. In humans, though, it came primarily in the form of lesions, scars, webbed-fingers, and their ilk.

But in Greg, it was his eyes that had changed. As he had grown older, they had begun to glow an unnatural yellow. Only his skills as a hunter and tracker had kept him from being outcast by those who shared his home. His eyes has also became super-sensitive to light, so much so that he had had to fashion thick, shaded goggles to even see in the light of the sun. At night, however, his vision was sharper than a cat's. That was why he had been chosen to hunt the beast this night.

Greg checked the rifle, making sure that there was a round ready in its chamber. He knew he was getting close to the thing's lair if the tracks were any indication. Suddenly, his horse reared, struggling against the reins. He fought to hold on, but the horse knocked him from his feet and then galloped off into the night. As he tried to pull himself up from the mud, the beast burst from the tree line, lopping towards him on all four legs like a wolf. He rolled from its path, swinging the rifle at its face. The gun shattered, leaving a patch of blood-matted fur on the creature's head. It staggered for a moment, dazed as Greg leapt up, drawing his knife from his belt. Then their eyes met. The thing's gaze was yellow like his own, glowing in the darkness. In that instant, Greg's world went white as a flash erupted inside his mind. He felt the wound on his head where his own gun had struck, and he ran on all fours through the forest, stopping only to hiss at the moon above. He felt powerful, alive, and hungry. He was nature's child and the forest was his and his alone.

Greg shook his head and found himself staring at the beast. It circled him slowly, a low rumble in its throat, yet it made no further advance. It knew he saw the truth. It had never been a bear or a cat: it was like him and he like it. They shared a kinship deeper than the bonds of man. Greg lowered his knife as it gave him one last look of pity before disappearing into the trees once more.

Greg felt his knees give way and fell back onto the muddy ground. A tear slid down his cheek, lost in the rain. He had failed his village, but he had found a new world that pulled at his heart, and he longed to be a part of it. Wondering who he really was and where his home truly lay, he looked up at the moon through the clouds. He howled, long and mournful.

The Devil's Ride

Blue lights reflected in the rearview mirror. Jack cursed, slamming his hands on the sides of the steering wheel as he checked his speed. The speedometer read 85 mph. For a second, Jack considered flooring the pedal, but he realized that running would only make things worse. The last thing he needed were more cops after him tonight, and there was a much easier and fun way to deal with the interloper. He slowed his speed and pulled onto the roadside. The highway was empty to the horizon in both directions except for the trooper's car, which pulled off behind him in the pale starlight of the desert night.

Jack reached for the cigarette that was dangling from the edge of the car's ashtray and took a long drag as he watched the trooper step out of his vehicle. He was a younger man, but not a stupid one. Jack could tell from the way he approached that the officer knew what he was doing. The trooper shined his flashlight over Jack's hands on the wheel.

Jack looked up smiling.

"Can I help you, officer?"

"License and registration," the trooper ordered.

Jack laughed and flicked his cigarette through the air at the man's face. Caught off guard, he stumbled as Jack slammed open his door, knocking him from his feet. In a blur, Jack was over him, pinning him to the ground. The trooper struggled, well-toned muscles rippling under his uniform, but Jack's grip was like steel.

Jack's tongue shot out. Impossibly long and ribbed with flecks of bone matter that seemed to grow out from inside the tissue, it tore into the young man's neck. Blood sprayed over Jack as the officer convulsed and spasmed below him. Jack shook his head and his tongue ripped free.

Black pus oozed from its entry point. Jack licked his lips unnaturally as his tongue folded back into his mouth.

When the officer lay still, Jack picked up his corpse effortlessly and carried him around to the trunk. He popped it open and tossed the trooper inside on top of his earlier prey, two unfortunate people working at a late-night roadside diner fifty miles back. Without a second thought, Jack closed the trunk and got back in the car. He lit another smoke and cranked up the radio as he peeled out and shot back onto the road. "Sympathy for the Devil" by the Stones blared into the night, and Mexico was only miles away.

The Rising

It all began with the plague. The dead rose from their tombs, spreading pestilence across the globe. I fought in the last battle to hold New York, watching the gray-skinned legions shamble mindlessly forward towards our lines. Maggots swam in their rotting flesh, and their ranks stretched and blurred into the horizon. Automatons though they were, they outnumbered us twenty to one even in those early days. The dull, horrible sound of their moaning had been so great that it could be heard over the cacophony of blazing weapons and the explosions of grenades that had been launched into their midst as they pushed through our barricades and broke free of the city proper.

The South fared no better, for down in the mountains of North Carolina, another evil stirred, and the wolves rose up on two legs to join the fight against mankind. What rumors we heard of Alaska and the Antarctic brought us an even greater fear of the darkness. In those places, it was said the dead were far from mindless. They were fast, cunning, and strong enough to rip through the steel walls of bases with bare hands, their red fangs glistening in the emergency lights.

No longer was humanity separated by such petty things as politics and faith. We stood together in an attempt to survive the new age dawning upon us. A choice was made to use the world's nuclear arsenals, and the great cities like New York, Moscow, London, and Berlin were the first to be scorched to nothing but radioactive dust. Atomic fire swept the streets of the dead and living alike; millions had perished.

From the bottom of the ocean, a new land rose above the tides, and upon its shores dwelled a race far older than our own. The few mariners who survived the horrors that the sea now held reported that, upon this land, the "Deep Ones" performed the last rituals to secure our demise and to awaken their long slumbering master, who was already stirring beneath the waves.

But all that is past now, as humanity soon shall be. I reside inside the concrete walls of this mighty bunker buried within the earth itself, along with soldiers like myself, guarding the leader of a democracy that is no more. We spend our remaining time listening to talons scraping the shelter's outer doors, or trying to tune in a radio frequency from another base like our own. We find only the croaking and chitterings of things from outside of time. Eventually, death will come for us, but for today we just hope that the doors hold. We pray and fight on.

To Be Born

I can still hear his breathing behind me, a wet sputtering noise. It takes me a moment to turn around, though I can't say why. Red bubbles pulsate over his lips as he tries to sit up and reach for the gun near his mangled form. I raise my own hand, and thunder floods the room with a flash. His head snaps back as the 9mm round shreds his brain. There's a dull thud, then the room is silent. I look around at the bodies of his guards. One lies broken in half near the door, two lie in puddles of red and are riddled with 9mm entry wounds, and the last lies facedown with his arms stretched out; there's a hole in the back of his head where my hand had punched through.

Smoke lingers around the barrel of my weapon, and I watch it drift away into the air. Fighting the desire to flee, to just run away, I walk calmly, stepping over the dead, out of the office onto the street. Sirens blare in the distance, but they have no meaning to me. I am above the law. Or so I am told.

Sometimes, I wonder what it is like to die. I imagine that's natural, given my relationship with death. What concerns me is that I have begun to wonder what it is like to be born.

I have never seen the sun rise. I have never made love to a woman, nor felt the comforting hand of a friend. My brothers and I do not talk. We are not allowed to. I listen to the technicians, though, as they tuck me into my vat at the end of each night. I listen to their worries, to their small talk, and I wonder what it is like to be them. They never speak to me. They clean away the blood, make needed repairs in my tissue, and place me inside my home. The suspending fluids pour in, and the blackness comes. I wonder if that sensation is what death is like: alone in the void with only your thoughts echoing in the emptiness.

I have never spoken a word that "they" did not give me, but I long to. I wish to ask Tech, designate: Carl, about his children and how little Michael is doing with his "cold." To ask Tech, designate: Terry, about her kitchen and to see if she has repaired the "grease-fire" damage. But I do not. I have seen what happens to, and have even eliminated, my brothers who have shown "thought." Perhaps soon, my brothers will have to deal with me.

I stand in the alley and watch the black van pull in, its door already sliding open. Agent, designate: Jason, motions me inside. I climb in and sit motionless, eyes staring forward, seeing nothing as we drive away. He and his partner, Agent, designate: John, will take me home to the lab now. I look forward to the vat and the void, for perhaps the blackness will amend these feelings. But if I awake again, John and Dennis will have no chance against me if I refuse to return again to the void. They were "born" and I was made. Made to kill for my country, though I am not sure I know what that is.

Summer Ending

Things crawl under his flesh, making his gray face ripple. Self-inflicted red and black tattoos of blood and Hell cover his hands as he straps me to the table. I want to scream, but only a ragged gasp leaves my throat. The cold touch of his skin burns me. I know without a shadow of a doubt that he is not dead, but neither is he alive. He is in-between. His human soul is gone, yet his mind and body live on. He has seen the horrors, the scorched earth above, and has made his home here in the depths of the old subways. I should have known better than to seek shelter down here, but the sky has gone dark once more, the temperatures well below freezing as a mixture of snow and ancient ash still rain from the heavens. He caught me there in the lightless tunnels, shivering and too weak to fight back, and he dragged me downward to his home.

He has the plague, the bug that killed so many before the sky-fire came. I can see them. In the thin, pale patches where his blue veins show through, I watch them dart by like flashes of nightmares. They call it the WORM in the old books. I can't imagine the pain he must be in. Yet I feel nothing for him because I am about to become his breakfast, lunch, and dinner. He'll feast on me for quite a while, rationing me out so that he need not go upwards again for weeks.

The only light comes from a torch, which flickers above the table that I am being bound to. My mind races, and my heart thunders in my chest. I have got to get free. With all my strength, I shove myself up from the tabletop and lash out with my free hand. My fist strikes his jaw, sending him reeling backwards. I suppose he thought I was too weak to resist. I tear my other hand free from the leather strap and lunge for the corner of the room where my gear lays. He has rifled through it, but being what he is, he didn't know or could not remember what to look for. I grab up the .45 and turn back to face him as he comes at me, yelling in anger and pain.

In a quick burst, I empty the remaining three rounds into his chest. The gun doesn't have the stopping power to down him. I meet him in his charge at me, slamming the butt of the gun into his temple. Bone cracks and he topples.

I don't bother to see if he is dead. I scoop up my gear and run out in the dusty, damp corridors. There is no sign of pursuit. After hours of bumbling about in the dark, I see the sky again. It is still black, but it is nowhere near as dark as the depths below.

I pull my heavy parka tighter about my body and throw my hood up over my head, stepping out into the howling winds. I pray that I can find shelter somewhere in the ruins of the city soon, because summer is ending, and the true winter draws nearer each day.

Julie's Dream

The storm was moving in fast. The first few drops of rain were beginning to fall. Lightning rippled and danced through the clouds above as Julie started to roll up the windows. Her car was a mess. The backseat was littered with paperbacks and magazines that she hadn't bothered to unload from the signing she'd done the night before.

Her signing had gone well by the standards of the town she lived in—here in the middle of nowhere North Carolina—and when she'd gotten home, she'd been too fired up to waste time on taking the books into the house. Instead, she'd rushed inside and headed straight to work. Her night had been spent in front of the computer in her study. She had searched the web for publishers outside of the sphere she normally worked in to submit her first novel to. She'd met with little success. It seemed that every publication was closed to submissions or unwilling to publish a book about the end of the world. Sinking into a funk, she ended up spamming some message boards with links to her latest short story collection.

At nearly thirty, Julie was widely published in the small press and literary journals. She had a small following of fans and was a minor local celebrity, but she wanted more. She didn't care about being the next Stephen King. All she wanted was some real recognition for her work outside of the small press. She'd spent the last three years of her life questing after it and felt defeated.

Exhausted from another pointless and sleepless night, she'd headed back out to the car and driven to her parents' old house as the sun rose. They were gone now. Cancer had claimed her father, and her mother had died in a car wreck last year. Their house was in a terrible state of disrepair because Julie never had time to deal with it after inheriting it. Yet she came here often to park in the driveway and stare at the vines that were growing up the weather-beaten walls, a notebook of blank pages spread open before her and leaning against the steering wheel.

Being at the house always made her pain of failure more intense as it reminded her that even if she succeeded her parents would never know. The pain fed her muse. At the best of times, it inspired her to crank out a few new tales in a single week, and at the worst, it sent her back to the ER with a fresh set of scars on her already razorblade-shredded wrists.

The storm was unexpected though. She cursed herself for being lazy the night before as she fought to keep her books safe from the downpour as the rain picked up. With the windows up, at last she settled back and listened to the rain thumping on the roof of the car. She reached up and ran a hand through her short brown hair and felt the scar tissue of her wrist brush lightly against the edge of her ear. She tossed the open notebook into the passenger seat and turned her gaze to the clouds.

The world outside the car had become as black as night. There had been a time in her life when faith was very important to her. She'd prayed to God every day about her dream of being a respected writer. Now, she imagined that if she ever met God she'd spit in the bastard's face. How long was she to bleed before he heard her crying so desperately to him?

Julie looked out through the waves of rain that were washing down the windshield. "Satan, father of the night," she found herself begging, "please grant me my dream and I will be yours."

Thunder crashed above her. She watched in stunned awe and growing terror as the clouds reshaped themselves into the face of the most beautiful man she'd ever beheld. The face smiled down at her.

"I hear your prayers, Julie. I am not like *him*," a voice purred in her mind. "What you ask shall be yours if you are still willing to bleed for it."

"Yes!" Julie screamed, her voice echoing inside the car.

Then, the storm cleared as quickly as it came. The sun blazed in a blue sky.

Julie felt something wet tickling down her arms as her fingers still dug into the steering wheel from the lingering moment of rapture in Lucifer's mental embrace. She let go of the wheel and looked at her wrists. All of her scars had reopened into fresh wounds. The blood poured so fast that it pooled in her lap even before she could yank open the car door and hurl herself outside to stand in the grass. Leaving a trail of red behind her, she staggered toward her parents' house with tears in her eyes. After only a few steps, she was too weak to continue and collapsed to her knees on the gravel drive. Her mind fought to explain what was happening as she grew lightheaded and toppled to the ground. Had Satan really spoken to her? She noticed she held a razor in one hand and watched the blood pumping from her wrists. She opened her mouth to cry out for help, to call to God for forgiveness. Nothing but a weak breath escaped her lips. Darkness flowed over her, and she saw flames flicker to life around her.

Two days later, when the local police found her body, partially eaten by wild dogs and decaying in the sun, the local papers contained an article about her suicide. Beside it was an article that had been written prior to the first. It was also about Julie. She had won the World Fantasy Award for her first novella, which had been published the year before.

Grave Watchers, Inc.

Steve gazed at the shotgun resting in his lap, a nervous unease eating away at him. He had never cared very much for firearms of any kind. He saw himself as a thinker, not a fighter. He ran a finger down the cold metal of the sawed-off barrel. There was no way out now, having come this far.

"Don't let the waiting get to you," Chris said flatly, his rotund form perched on a nearby tombstone that barely supported his weight. He wore a horribly out-of-fashion shirt with colors so bright that they hurt Steve's eyes. His black jeans were splattered with mud and his hair was black with a hint of gray, so oily it glistened in the rays of the setting sun.

Steve looked around at the grave markers, which were so worn by time that few still possessed any readable markings. "Yeah," Steve answered, pushing his glasses back into place with a single thin finger. The things had a bad habit of sliding down his face but he didn't have the cash to get a new pair. His own hair was a disheveled mess of blond atop his head, and he wore an old ratty Alien Sex Fiend T-shirt. Always self-conscious, he tugged at its back uncomfortably.

The old Fairview cemetery: that's what people called this place. It had been filled beyond its limits and abandoned years ago. Still, even backwoods places like this needed to be guarded if the town were to avoid the plague that was claiming the world as its own.

"How did you get into this line of work?" Steve asked.

Chris shook his M-16 at Steve. "You mean this?"

Steve nodded.

"I founded Grave Watchers, son, three months ago with a friend of mine named John. Remember when the first reports from up north began to show up on every station and the shit really hit the fan? The local newscasters not really believing the reports they were reading?"

Again Steve nodded, wishing Chris would get to the point.

"Well, when John and I saw those reports, we were sitting on the couch in my living room, bullshitting and being pissed off about the Sunday game being interrupted. We got drunk." Chris laughed, the mounds of his flesh rolling with the movement.

"We started asking ourselves if what was happening up there could happen down here in the south, too. At first, we were scared shitless, but then we started thinking: maybe, just maybe, down here it could be stopped before it ever started . . . if someone were to watch the graveyards and morgues, and put those bastards back down into Hell before they got loose. John and me, well, we were both ex-military, so we ran an ad in the papers to do just that. We got more responses from mayors and city officials than we knew what to do with, so the company was born. Our fees were monstrous, but this is a monstrous job. We hired on extra help, had to, from job to job, and a few permanents.

"Now we're covering more than six counties, kid. You're going to be real happy with your paycheck when we get out of here, if you handle yourself well enough and don't get careless."

"Has . . . has anyone ever been killed doing this?" Steve stammered, looking away from Chris's stare.

"Sure. It happens in almost every job, kid," Chris chuckled when he saw Steve's trembling hands, the knuckles growing white from the grip he had on his rifle. "Only the stupid and unlucky get ate or infected. Those who set up for the job in the wrong place where some of those things could flank 'em or bravado-filled punks with balls too big for their own good. They're the ones that die." Chris waved a hand through the air in a gesture of confidence. "We ain't got nothin' to worry about here. Fairview's so old I doubt any of 'em will even be intact enough to wake up."

Chris stared at Steve, who seemed to be fighting some kind of inner battle with himself, blinking when Steve's 12-guage was thrust within an inch of his forehead. He looked up the barrel in disbelief as Steve stood above him.

"Which kind of punk was my father?" Steve asked, his voice filled with anger and hard determination.

"Damn, I thought you looked kind of familiar. He was on that job up in Canton, wasn't he? We lost of a lot of good men up there."

Steve pumped a round into the chamber. "What happened?"

"We weren't prepared. It was one of our first big jobs, ya see? I don't think a lot of people took it seriously. Sometimes ya can't believe something like this without seeing it with your own eyes. Hundreds and hundreds of those things dug themselves up all around us, wave after wave. Everybody panicked. We all got separated in the chaos. If it hadn't been for John's radio, none of us would've gotten out of there alive. As it was, we were barely able to hold the things long enough for the National Guard to show up."

"Good answer," Steve grinned, letting the gun drop a bit. "But you still let it happen," he said, jerking the gun back up and squeezing the trigger. Chris's face was torn to shreds by the scattershot weapon, bits of blood and bone rained onto the ground around the tombstone he sat on. His almost headless corpse tottered for a moment, then fell with a loud thump to the dirt.

Steve fell to his knees, smearing the blood that had spattered on his face with the back of his sweaty hand. Tears burned in his eyes. "Bastard," Steve sobbed. "You lousy bastard. You shouldn't have let it happen."

In that moment, he did not hear the low sound of muffled moaning around him. He paid no attention to the first hand as it tore through the dirt not five feet from where he sat, its decaying fingers grasping at the air. Steve never moved, he only wept. He cried and cried—and screamed.

The Last Man

You would think that being the last man on earth would be fun. Hell, maybe it *would* be if the damned dead stayed in their graves. The fantasy of being chased by a mob of ladies takes on a different tone when their flesh is gray and decayed and they want your body for the literal taste of its blood and meat.

I should have know better than to break into the women's prison, but, *damn*, it's like twenty degrees in the sun and the snow is still falling. So, I break off the lock on the main gates and start heading in, dreaming of a roof over my head and of watching furniture burn in a warm fire. But I freeze as women pour into the prison yard like kids who have just seen the ice cream truck pull up. I stand there with the broken lock in my hands and watch them come.

At last, my mind snaps out of it and I jerk my 9mm from its holster. A few well-placed shots splatter the brains of the closest three, staining the snow a blackish red. There's no way I can take them all down. I guess they number above four dozen in all. Turning my back to them, I hightail it towards the forest outside the gates. Why the hell couldn't all the movies about slow zombies be right? I wonder as they sprint after me, their nearly frozen joints popping.

When I reach the trees, I risk a look back. One of them, a blonde missing her lower jaw, is right there in my face. In a panic, I grab her by the hair and slam her head into the bark of the nearest tree until my hands are soaked with the black crap that passes for the blood of the dead. I drop her corpse and look up to see that the others are only a few feet away, closing fast. No time to take another shot at them with the pistol.

Again, I'm running, dodging trees and leaping over logs, limbs, and brush. I zigzag through the woods, hoping that if I get out of the line of sight, they'll lose me. No such luck. The damn things are like bloodhounds with the smell of warm flesh. I plunge my hand into the pocket of my heavy coat as I pant and pump my legs. I pull out my only grenade, looted from the body of a half-eaten soldier a few towns back, and I pull out the pin, tossing the bomb over my shoulder. It lands too close. The force of the explosion throws me and sends me rolling.

When I come to a stop, I leap to my feet despite the searing pain in my back. I hold my 9mm ready. Pieces of several ladies twitch in the snow not far away. The rest of the pack comes trampling over them. I empty my clip in a series of thunderclaps, drowning out their hungry howling.

Oh yeah, great fun to be the last man, I think as the first one woman tackles me and we go sprawling.

When the ladies pour over me, I don't scream. Instead, I find myself laughing as their mouths rip through my clothes and find what they seek. I keep right on laughing until a set of yellow teeth tears out my vocal cords, until I'm just as cold as they are and the warmth of my parka no longer matters.

Shadows

Lois was awakened by something soft and gentle pressing lightly against her forehead. She did not open her eyes. The room stunk of death, of decay so putrid that it made her gag. She knew if she opened her eyes he would be there, looming above her. Goose bumps formed on her skin as her heart stiffened inside her chest. Her breath came in heavy, frightened gasps.

Out in the kitchen, Jeannie called out for the fourth time. "Damn it!" She had enough problems without dealing with the brat, too. Jeannie was a single mother and it was all she could do to keep going from one day to the next. Lois had always been John's daughter more than hers. Lois was a true "daddy's girl" who blamed her for John leaving. They fought nearly every day about it. This morning, though, Jeannie didn't have time for it. She was sick of listening to the brat rattle on and on about her crazy dreams of her father. The damn car was acting up again. Its transmission was on its last legs, and Jeannie herself had gotten up late. Her head throbbed from her morning hangover, and she felt like shit. Still, there was nothing to do for it. She had to go to work and get the brat to school on time. Jeannie cursed again and threw the pan of frying eggs at Lois's bedroom door. It struck with a loud thump, cracking the flimsy wood.

Lois heard her mother yelling but didn't move. The icy finger removed itself from her forehead and she heard the rustling of rags as the thing of her nightmares slunk away from her. She was only eight years old but she knew the truth of things more than her mother did. Daddy hadn't left them. He died in an accident almost a year ago, and he came back to visit every night and every morning. She was sure he did it out of love, but he still scared the hell out of her. The dead weren't supposed to drop by for visits.

Jeannie ripped open the door to Lois's room and stood in the doorway, staring at her with bloodshot eyes. "Get up you little bitch! We're going to be late!"

Lois opened her eyes and threw down her covers. Daddy was gone. She swung her feet over the edge of the bed and leaned down to reach for her clothes, but Jeannie stormed over to Lois and yanked her to her feet by her hair. Lois cried out in pain and tears welled up in her eyes, streaming down her cheeks. She looked up at Jeannie and whimpered. "I'm sorry mommy, but daddy—"

"That's it!" Jeannie roared and backhanded Lois so hard she knocked the girl back onto her bed. "I've had enough of your crap! Daddy's gone and he ain't comin' back, no matter how much you cry about it!"

Lois saw him then standing behind her mother, blacker than midnight in the tattered rags that served as his death shroud and heavy cloak. Instead of eyes, twin orbs of red burned inside the empty sockets of his skeletal face. He had whispered to her many times before about what Hell was like, but Lois never fully understood except for when she saw him like this.

"Jesus!" Jeannie said, catching a whiff of his odor as it crept back into the room. "What have you done in here? Did you shit the bed, you little bitch?"

Lois didn't answer. She could only stare at her father with a mixture of awe, love, and fear.

He spoke then, a single word: "Jeannie." His voice was hollow and sounded like the sharp hiss of air leaving a ruptured lung.

Jeannie froze in place. Lois couldn't help but smile a bit. Now, mommy would have to believe her.

Daddy leaned forward, one of his unnaturally long arms wrapping around Jeannie's neck from behind. Jeannie's face had gone pale and she started to scream, howling at the top of her lungs. Daddy's cloak enveloped Jeannie's body as he pulled her even closer. Jeannie thrust her elbow backwards like she'd learned in self-defense class. It struck bone, shattering the specter's ribs and tearing its dark rags. But the thing didn't release her or even soften its grip. Jeannie erupted into a mass of swinging limbs as it lifted her from the floor.

"Little bitch?" the thing hissed. "You are the bitch, Jeannie."

Lois watched as her daddy poked one of his bony fingers into Jeannie's throat. Blood spurted from the wound as the finger slowly raked its way across Jeannie's neck. Then, daddy dropped her spasming body to the floor and showed his white teeth to Lois, vanishing into the shadows.

Lois heard shouts from the hallway as Mr. Allen kicked down the front door. He rushed into her bedroom to see her sitting calmly upon her bed. Below her dangling feet, Jeannie's corpse lay on the floor in an ever-widening pool of red.

The Inside

Rain fell on the roof in the gentle pattern that often guides insomniacs into the world of long sought sleep. Ben would find no sleep this night, nor did he care for the rain, no matter how beautiful and peaceful it sounded. He lay in his bed, covers thrown askew, drenched in sweat from his unrest and from the humidity of the hot summer night. The dim glow of his alarm clock was a constant reminder that he should have been long asleep.

Tonight was his last night at home. Time had crept up on him. Tomorrow, he would leave never to return; college, a place of his own, even if it was a crowded and cramped dorm room, loomed before him. Yet, it was not thoughts of his future that kept him awake. He stared at the white tiles of the ceiling, listening to his nightly tormentor, the soft scraping and scratching of tiny feet, wondering how after all the years there was any ceiling left between them.

His whole life, he had been haunted by nightmares of the thing that lurked up there in the crawlspace between the ceiling and the actual roof. Fear was an emotion Ben came to know intimately, from the early days of childhood to this very moment. He wished feverishly he could convince himself the creature was a phantom conjured up by his own imagination, but he knew the creature was real.

Other people had heard the awful clawing and pitter-patter of tiny feet rushing about above his bed. People like his own mother, to whom he had ran as a child. "Mom, the monster's back!" he would cry. "It's coming to get me." His mother would always take his hand and lead him calmly back to bed. As she tucked him in tightly, she would whisper in his ear, reassure him it was only a baby bird from a nest in the crawlspace that hadn't yet took flight. Or, at worst, a rat that she would promptly take care of in the morning. Her story changed from time to time, but in the light of day, she did ascend a ladder to the dark place, littering it with traps and various poisons. Perhaps over the years she became lost in her own form of denial, for the noise never went away.

Tonight, the claws dug with a fresh zeal, as if somehow sensing that Ben would soon be gone. Remembering the nights spent under the covers, remembering the hell of sleeping only at the creature's whim, Ben let his anger grow deep and burning.

He climbed out of bed, clad only in a pair of ancient boxers, stumbling his way through lightless hallways to the kitchen. Only after quietly shutting the kitchen door did he turn on a light, trying hard not to disturb his parents. With care, he selected the tools he would need: a sharp, stainless steel knife that his mother used for cutting meat and a wooden broom with a long handle. He cursed the fact that no one in the house owned a gun; it would have made things so much simpler, but his mother would not tolerate such an instrument of death under her roof while she still breathed. Broom and knife in hand, Ben tiptoed to his room and gently shut the door behind him.

He switched on the lamp, laying the knife beside it on the white dresser, which had helped him through so many nights before. Steadying himself for a moment, he muttered a prayer to a god in whom he didn't fully believe. Then, he stepped up onto his bed, mattress bouncing slightly under his weight.

The noise had faded. Maybe the thing realized what he intended. Nonetheless, he waited, broom poised towards the ceiling. He didn't have to wait long. As soon as the scratching began, he rammed the broom upwards at an angle, dislodging the tile, which fell with his monster to the floor below. Ben leapt off the bed, half expecting to find the rat of which his mother spoke. He found instead a creature with the writhing body of a snake, its slick scales disrupted here and there by patches of ragged, putrid fur. Though less than a foot tall, it pulled itself up on pale infant-like legs. Its tiny yellow eyes stared at Ben, boring into his soul. "What are you?" he blurted, unable to stop himself.

Black decaying teeth parted in the hideous parody of a smile. "Don't you recognize yourself?" the creature hissed.

Ben snapped out of his trance. Forgetting the knife on the dresser, he swung the broom handle down upon the abomination. The creature squealed in pain. Again and again Ben struck amid its pleas for mercy. With blood flowing from its deformed ears and from the corners of its yellow eyes, it vainly attempted to fend off the blows. Never once did it strike back.

When his parents, alerted by a crash, burst into the room, they found their son sitting motionless in a pool of blood—with the broken and battered body of a rat clutched in his hands. Ben spent the rest of his life as a hollow shell, resting in a sterile white asylum bed.

Coins

The night was late and the day had been the busiest for the store in ages. Lisa sat in the back office at her desk, counting down the cash drawers. Tomorrow was the big day. Ralph was coming to inspect the store and evaluate her for the management position. If things went well, she'd finally be on a salary instead of a lousy $6.50-an-hour wage.

She watched Chris on the security monitor and cursed the little punk as he struggled to shelve the day's returns. She guessed it had never occurred to him that working in a video store would be so much work. His face was contorted in pain as he carried stack after stack of videos to their shelves. He suffered from a rare spinal disease that would someday twist his spine enough to shut down his kidneys.

Lisa watched as he tossed aside the stack he carried and stormed back toward the office door. He threw it open and stood before her, face red and eyes filled with anger. "I'm going home," he said.

"Did I give you permission to clock out?" Lisa snarled.

"No, but I told my parents I would be home by midnight. It's nearly 3 AM. I'm leaving." Chris turned his back on her and headed out of the office, time card in hand.

Lisa leapt up from her chair and grabbed him, shoving him so hard that he fell to the floor. He looked up at her with hatred. "What the hell's your problem, bitch?"

"What did you call me?" She dropped on top of him, straddling his struggling form. "You little bastard!" she wailed as something snapped inside her. "I'll teach you to talk back to me!" She grabbed a roll of pennies from a nearby drawer and rammed it into his mouth, shoving it around like a bar of soap. Chris gagged and tried to knock her off, but his back hurt and his arms had little strength left. His teeth bit into the roll as he fought to breathe. The spit-soaked paper shredded and the roll broke open, raining metal down his throat and closing off his air way. His eyes burned with tears as the pennies cut into the insides of his throat.

Thinking his increased struggling was against her, Lisa pounded him with her fists until they came away soaked in blood. Only when Chris laid still, his eyes bulging and his skin blue, did Lisa realize what had happened. She vomited onto his corpse as it grew cold under her. Through tears of her own, it sunk in that now she'd never get the promotion. Her sobs grew heavier as she leaned over and buried her head against his unmoving chest.

Loose

Shannon woke to the beeping of the alarm clock. As he reached over Brook to shut it off, she stirred, rolling over to glance up at him with sleepy eyes. He leaned down to kiss her gently on the forehead before he climbed out of bed and slipped out of the room. Feeling his way through the early morning darkness of the hallway, he made his way to the bathroom for a quick shower. His red uniform shirt and black jeans lay crumpled on the tile floor where he had discarded them the night before. After he showered, he put the clothes back on. On days like this, when he opened the morning after closing the store, he never felt he had a lot of time and was forced to make due.

His apartment, like all those in Cavalier Arms, was roughly "L" shaped with the long part of the "L" leading straight back into the bathroom and with the doors to the guest bedroom and the main bedroom to its left and right. At the other end of the "L" shape lay a small kitchen area and living room. Shannon stumbled down the hall into the kitchen, still feeling only half awake despite his shower. His work hours at the video store had been long the last few days and were beginning to take their toll. Two members of the store's tiny staff had recently quit, and he found himself picking up all the slack. It didn't seem fair, but he was up for a promotion and didn't want to do anything to hurt his chances.

He opened the refrigerator door, searching for a quick and easy breakfast. Nothing caught his eye. He closed the door and decided to pick up something on the way to work. He yanked his jacket off the back of a chair at the kitchen table and headed out into the morning chill. Winter hadn't quite loosened its hold on the mountains yet.

Cavalier Arms was a low-income housing project set up by the government, and its parking lot was well lit by numerous streetlights. There were twelve buildings that ran the length of the lot on either side, each containing two apartments. Shannon's silver Dodge Shadow was parked beside the large green dumpsters of the complex. He walked towards the driver's door, fishing around in his pocket for the keys.

Something thumped loudly from inside the closest dumpster. Shannon figured it was just one of the neighborhood cats again; they often got inside to find food and were unable to get out. But as the sound came again, the whole massive dumpster shook as if something far larger than any cat were moving around inside. Shannon backed off a couple of steps and gawked as a creature emerged from the dumpster as if crawling from a nightmare. It pulled itself up over the edge and leapt to the pavement in front of him. It stood only about three feet tall with sleek gray reptilian scales covering its naked form. Its body was a mass of what looked to be pure muscle tissue, and long talons stretched from where its fingers should have been. Hunger burned in its yellow eyes. It snarled at Shannon as he broke into a run for his apartment. Shannon wasn't fast enough. The thing landed on his back, tearing into him with its large claws. Shannon screamed as the thing sunk its teeth into his neck, and he toppled to the pavement under the thing's weight. Shannon's body lay in a pool of his own blood as the thing continued to rip and shred his flesh.

***

Lucas sat beside the window of his apartment, smoking and watching the scene. Mary staggered up to him, wearing pajamas and rubbing her eyes. "What's going on?".

Lucas didn't answer. Mary glanced out the window over Lucas and saw Shannon's corpse and the thing outside. "Jesus, Lucas! What the Hell is going on?"

Lucas took a long drag from his cigarette. "I don't have the faintest," he answered her with wide eyes.

"Oh God, you've got to help him, Lucas."

"What?" Lucas mumbled, so stunned he nearly dropped his cigarette.

"Get out there and help him, you lazy bastard!"

Lucas stared at her. "You help him, you crazy bitch. I ain't goin' out there."

Mary ran down the hall to their bedroom and returned with one of Lucas's .45 automatics in her hand. Aside from being the "super" of the complex, Lucas was a drug dealer. He kept quite a few guns on hand, in case a deal should ever go sour. He watched as Mary slung open their outer door. She started shooting the second she was outside. Bullets sparked and pinged off the parking lot near the creature. It dropped the part of Shannon it had been gnawing on and darted at her. Her first successful round caught it square in the face. The creature flew from its feet, but Mary never stopped firing. She kept her pace towards the thing, pulling the trigger over and over until the .45 clicked empty. By the time she reached the creature, its body lay twitching on the ground, riddled with holes that leaked black, pus-like fluid.

Lights were coming on all over the complex now. Bo, an elderly African American gentleman who had come outside to help, hurried to Mary's side. He helped her roll Shannon over and nearly vomited when he saw what was left of Shannon's face.

A crowd gathered around them. Melissa was there with her three year old clinging to her blouse. Hank from apartment fourteen shook his head at the mess. Everyone was full of questions and wondered what the hell the thing was that had killed Shannon. Only Ms. Johnson stood apart from the crowd. She sobbed loudly and wiped at the tears that poured from her wrinkled eyes. She left them all there wondering and went back inside her apartment. She walked slowly to her back room and stared at the broken chains on her son's bedroom wall. "Oh, Timothy, I'm so sorry." She cried and collapsed to the floor. She picked up a bone on which Timothy had been sharpening his teeth the night before and cradled it as the sun rose over Cavalier Arms.

The Takers

It was the day before Thanksgiving, but Mark had little to be thankful for. As he drove away from his home, he replayed their last conversation in his head: "There are givers and takers, Mark," she'd said. "You can't have one without the other. And I'm through giving." He had said everything he could think of to keep the ship from going down, but it didn't matter. The marriage was over.

In a way, he blamed himself for not caring enough. Maybe she was right, but she'd known what he was like when she married him. He was meant for greater things—if she could just see that, that the times he ignored her were an investment in the future...

When he thought about it, the divorce just seemed like one of those things that were meant to be, part of his weird destiny. He supposed when the initial shock wore off, he would hurt a great deal more. But right now, he had other things to worry about. Where would he live? Who would take care of him?

He had no steady income to speak of. He was a writer just beginning his career. Sometimes he sold short stories or articles for cash but most of the time he only got paid in copies and exposure. Even in his best months, he was lucky if he cleared two hundred dollars.

He reached down and flipped on the radio, hoping music would help calm him down and take his mind off his problems, but all could find across the dial was news. America was in a new war and there was no end in sight. He hoped there wouldn't be a draft. He already had enough problems in his life, and he didn't have time for distractions like that.

Mark left the radio on a random station and gunned the car, increasing his speed as he tore around the winding curves towards town. He realized that, without really thinking about it, he had decided to head for his parents' house. They wouldn't be happy to see him on their doorstep with his suitcases, but he could swallow his pride, and they would give him a place to stay. His mom wasn't as good a cook as his wife, but at least the laundry would get done.

While he sat behind the wheel, his mind was far away, making plans. He didn't notice until it was too late how close he was driving to edge of the road. His right front wheel dropped on the asphalt, sending him careening out of control. He fought to stabilize the car, tugging at the wheel with all his strength, but his speed was too great. The car flew from the road and smashed into a nearby tree as Mark's world went black.

He awoke with blood burning his eyes. He reached up to wipe it away, and a sharp stabbing pain shot through his body. Looking up at the shattered glass of the windshield where his forehead had struck, he realized that though his seat belt had saved his life, it had also fractured several of his ribs. He painfully slipped it off and opened the door, falling out onto the damp grass of the roadside.

He propped himself up against the car and fished around in his pocket for a cigarette. When he managed to get the pack out, he threw it away in disgust. The pack was soaked in blood.

He had no idea how long he had been out, but assumed it had been quite a while, as the sky was beginning to darken. Everything seemed gray, and he wondered if he was going to get rained on now, as well. Great.

Mark wondered why no one had came along and seen the accident. Surely if someone had, they would've stopped to try and help him. People still helped each other out, didn't they?

Suddenly, Mark heard laughter on the car radio. Mark leaned his body closer towards the car's open door to listen. How in the hell had the thing stayed on?

"Mark, Mark, Mark," the announcer laughed. "It's time to pay up, little brother."

Mark shook his head and thought he must be losing his mind. In the past few hours, he'd been through enough to push anyone over the edge. He thought he recognized the announcer's voice though; it was one he had not heard in years.

"Greg?" Mark mumbled to himself.

"Yep, it's me," the radio answered.

Mark stared at the dashboard in horror. He felt his heart sink inside his chest and tears began to well up in his eyes, washing the blood from his cheeks. "Greg . . . I am so sorry."

"I should think so," the radio voice answered in a cheerful tone. "You never come and visit me anymore. Why is that?"

"I, um, I guess I felt bad..." Mark was confused. Didn't Greg remember?

"About what, Mark? That I couldn't offer you anything else? You know, I was just reminiscing—remember when you showed up that day? It was the happiest day of my life:my long lost brother coming out of the blue after all those years apart. Do you remember how I hugged you?"

"It wasn't my fault..."

"Whose was it? Dad's, for spoiling you so much, I guess, getting you used to having your way. I gave you everything I had, and you took more. I got you a job, gave you a place to stay. It's not everyone who can take another person's whole life, Mark. You took my career, my wife, everything I had. "

"I didn't mean for it to happen the way it did, Greg," Mark whispered.

"Sure you didn't." Greg smiled, suddenly materializing in front of Mark's eyes on the road. The pale starlight of the night seemed to pass through Greg as if he weren't completely there. He leaned over and offered a translucent hand to Mark. "Just like you didn't mean to throw them away when you were done."

***

Sobbing, Mark looked away and ignored Greg's offer to help him to his feet. Mark began to feel an anger stirring inside of him. "It was your own fault, Greg."

"It was *my* fault that you were a drunk and a loser with nowhere else to go? I tried to help you, Mark. Is that why you murdered me? Hacked me up, tossed me in the trunk, and hauled me out here into the middle of nowhere?"

For the first time, Mark looked around. Greg was buried not twenty feet from where he sat, but that didn't matter now. "Yes!" Mark screamed turning to look into Greg's hollow eyes. "What you had should've been mine! It was *mine!* I didn't ask to be dragged away as a child. I wanted to stay with Mom, too. This town was my home!"

"Well," Greg said, "I don't guess it matters now, does it? Your wife—my wife, actually—was right, you know: there *are* givers and takers, and you can't have one without the other." Greg paused, glancing off into the woods. "They'll be here soon."

"Who? Who will be here soon?" Mark raged.

"The Takers," Greg watched the tree line, waiting. "I'd really love to stay and watch but not even the dead are safe from them. And I've given you enough. You won't get my soul, too."

Mark blinked as a drop of blood from his mangled scalp dripped into his eyes. By the time his eyes opened, Greg was gone. He was alone in the night.

Finding strength in his hatred of Greg, Mark pulled himself to his feet, using the car to lean on. "Come back, you bastard! We're not through yet! I killed you once, and by God, I can do it again!"

His voice echoed down the desolate roadway among the surrounding trees. Then he saw them, two black forms far in the distance. They stood on two legs like men, but the similarity ended there. Their arms were elongated, and their hands hung so low that the silver talons of their fingers scraped on the asphalt as they approached.

They were darker than the night and appeared to absorb all the light around them. The car's headlights flickered and died as they drew near. But their eyes glowed like the fires of hell, orange and bright, full of anger and hunger. Yellow teeth gleamed hungrily when they opened their mouths to howl. Mark grew cold as they approached, and his argument with Greg was forgotten. His worries from the day vanished, snatched from him and drawn into their shadowy forms. He couldn't remember even his wife's name, all of his memories gone, and he was left with nothing but the hollow emptiness of terror.

"Oh G-God," Mark heard himself stutter. He fell into the driver's seat and tore frantically at the glove compartment until he got it open. He pulled out a .38 revolver and hobbled up out of the car.

They were so close now he could smell the foul odor of brimstone and decay. Mark pointed the gun at them with his trembling hand, not even remembering now why they had come, but desperate to escape them. "I don't know who you are, but you don't have any business here." He pulled the gun's hammer back with his thumb. The beings paid no attention to his threats and continued their slow advance.

"Go away!" Mark wailed and fired. His bullet passed through the first creature and imbedded itself in a tree across the road with a soft whacking sound. He turned to run, but stopped, unsure of his way and unable to decide on a path.

"No!" Mark pleaded, finally running, but they were upon him. Their talons tore flesh and their yellow teeth gnawed upon his throat, but the physical pain was subdued, unreal compared to the feeling of having his being dragged from his tattered remains.

Greg watched them turn away as Mark's lifeless body sunk to the road. The lead creature held a small ball of light clutched in its paw as the pair melted into the darkness once more.

"Enjoy their company, Mark," Greg said. "You've earned it." Then he, too, was gone.

A gentle breeze picked up the fall leaves from Greg's unmarked grave. The leaves swirled into the air, but only Mark's soulless shell was left to see them reflecting in its glazed-over eyes.

Jesse Wept

As he checked the chamber of his Colt, Jesse took a long drag from the cigarette dangling between his lips. He slammed the full chamber into the gun and spun it, watching the dark streets below his window.

The dirty sheets on the bed were still turned up and unruffled. He would find no rest in this cheap excuse for a hotel tonight. Through the dusty windowpane, orange flames flickered in the night on the edge of town, casting eerie shadows across the room. If Jesse squinted hard enough, he could see the shadow things out there, dancing around the burning church.

X'ah had followed him here, and soon this quiet little town would be fighting for its life. Even now, Jesse imagined Reon's residents being dragged from their beds by X'ah's creatures, their flesh rent from their bones by the demons' razor-sharp claws—their despair as their physical bodies were eaten alive while their very souls were consumed by invisible mouths.

A shotgun thundered somewhere down the street from the hotel. Horses reared and kicked out against the walls of their pens. The animals felt the evil as deeply as he did. He should not have come here. The blood being shed in the darkness was upon his hands.

He wondered why he'd come. Perhaps in search of protection? Some vain hope that mankind could, or would, rise up to save him as he had for them time and again? But he realized with certainty that, in coming to Reon, he'd only brought death to their door. They could do nothing to help him—the limbless preacher dangling from the steeple of the church across the street was proof of that. The destruction of Reon would do nothing but buy him a few precious moments to prepare for what lay ahead.

Jesse tossed the butt of the cigarette aside and pulled another from the tin in his shirt pocket, striking a match against the room's rough wooden wall. There would be no more running. It would end here, tonight.

The door to his room burst open, nearly ripped from its hinges. Matthew, the fat hotelkeeper, barged in. He was sweating like a pig, and his skin burned a deep red from fright and exertion. "Mister, you better clear out! There are things out there in the street! They ain't human, killing everything in their path. They're working their way through the whole town!"

"I reckon' if I was you, I'd be runnin' then," Jesse smiled. Matthew stared at him for a second, befuddled by his calmness, and then shook his head, vanishing back out into the hall. Jesse listened to his shouts as he roused his other guests.

The streets below Jesse's window were alive now. Six-guns and rifles barked in the darkness, their short bursts a sharp contrast to the longer cries of the wounded and dying. Dark shapes flowed from the shadows and back into them, unhindered by the gunfire. Several other buildings were aflame now, and the town outside the window reminded Jesse of Richmond a few years before. He felt helpless like he had then. But maybe this time he could save the men from the Dark, as he couldn't save them from each other.

With a quick blow from the butt of one his twin revolvers, Jesse shattered the window and took aim at one of the moving shadows below. The gun's muzzle flashed, and the shot was followed by a shriek, high pitched and monstrous. A white body materialized and fell with a thud onto the walkway of the general store across the street. The thing was barely four feet tall and hairless from head to toe. It wore no clothes, and a yellow puss leaked from the wound on its scalp as its body twitched and thrashed about in the throes of death.

"X'ah!" Jesse shouted, "I'm here! Come out and face me like a man!"

Shadows moved and leapt. Dark forms hurried through the chaos below toward the window and the hotel. Jesse opened up, blazing away with his Colts. White demons suddenly appeared as they died, littering the streets.

Jesse's Colts clicked empty. He flung the chambers open, spent cartridges clattering onto the floor.. Quickly, he packed six silver rounds into each of the twin chambers. He kissed each of the chambers, a gentle, patient blessing.

"J-E-S-S-E," a voice colder than the deadest winter echoed in the hotel below. Jessie could hear an army of tiny feet climbing the stairs. The Devil didn't believe in a fair fight. Neither did Jessie, not this time. He climbed out the window, tossing his cigarette under his bed. As he half jumped, half fell to the street below, his room exploded in a shower of broken wood and flames. He heard the squeals of the demon things behind him as they died in the blast. "It's amazing what a few well-placed pounds of TNT can do," he laughed to himself.

He rolled with his fall, barely avoiding broken legs as he hit the ground. He was on his feet and running even as the hotel buckled inward on itself in a fiery collapse. He didn't delude himself with the notion that he'd been lucky enough to get X'ah, too. At best, he'd merely evened the odds.

Reon's survivors still ran about in the streets, panicked and terrified. A few had managed to find horses or wagons and were hotfooting it out of town. The Shadow things were there also, though their numbers were smaller, patches of blackness descending upon the innocents as they tried to flee.

Jesse stumbled in his haste for the stables and went tumbling into the dirt. Cursing loudly, he got to his feet as he saw the glowing figure of X'ah standing outside the remains of the hotel. A halo of light surrounded X'ah, and though the angel should have been beautiful in his white robes, the effect was marred by the glistening blood of the damned that dripped off of him. His eyes held an infinite blackness, and long blonde hair spilled down over his shoulders. He stood with his arms spread wide, as if to embrace the carnage before him.

"Jesse," his voice called out though his lips never moved. "It is time."

Jesse stood his ground, his hands resting on the butts of his holstered Colts.

"Go back to hell and leave me alone!" Jesse screamed, tears welling up in his eyes.

"Not without you." X'ah floated an inch off the ground as he swept towards Jesse. "Not without my son."

"I am not your son!" With blinding speed, Jesse's Colts cleared their holsters, but X'ah merely waved his hand, and the guns flew from Jesse's grasp.

Jesse turned to run, but X'ah was upon him, his arms snaking around him with blinding speed. "Are you not?" the demon asked as he drew the man close to him. Jesse struggled, but was helpless in the tentacled embrace. X'ah turned the man around, deposited him on the ground before him. "Are you not?" he repeated. "And who else would have you? The Creator?"

Jesse looked up, tears etching channels on his soot darkened face. He said nothing.

"Oh, yes, and will the Creator come and claim you as his offspring, haul you down from the tree where you hang amongst thieves and criminals? You made that mistake before, did you not? How many fathers will you call upon before you recognize me?"

Jess stubbornly shook his head. The demons surrounded him, visible now, leaving off their sport with the humans and leering at him maliciously. "You cannot be my father."

"Cannot? How can I *not* be your sire? Again I ask you, how many times will you be reborn, how many times will you give yourself to these sheep, calling on whatever new god they hold dear to recognize you? Did Zeus save you when you were chained to the rock, as I came every day to feed upon your liver? Will you give away more palaces, more riches, more kingdoms? Who else came for you—

Brahma? How many incarnations will you have, Lughnasadh? Or shall I call you Adonis, or Tammuz, or Enkidu or Quetzalcoatl?"

Jesse said nothing, defiance on his face, despair in his heart.

"Who is there with you, son of man, at every death? Who is the father of the Hanged Man if not the Devil?"

Jesse wept. "Enough," he said. "It is as you say. What do you want of me?"

The demon leaned forward, eagerly. The stench of ten million corpses was in his breath as he stretched forward to embrace his "son."

"Finally, you will acknowledge me?"

"No." The voice came from behind X'ah, and the demon whirled around, dragging the unfortunate gunslinger with him.

"Who dares?" he started.

A small girl-child stood there, tattered and dirty in her nightdress, ash on her face. "No!" she shouted up at X'ah. "You let him go!"

Jesse clamped his eyes shut, desperately praying to whatever god might be watching this generation, praying to the child. *Run, child, run.* "Leave her, X'ah, you have me."

Snaking his tentacles toward the child, X'ah released Jesse, who slumped to the ground. "I have you both, Jesse. And this one I will enjoy."

"No! Mama says you can't hurt me, not when my angel is watching. I know who you are, old Scratch. You have to go, 'cuz my friend's tougher than you."

X'ah caressed the girl's face, dragging his tentacle along her cheek. "Really, child? And who is your friend that he is so tough?"

"*He* is." She was pointing to Jesse, who was standing again. He had quickly looked for his guns, but realized now that he didn't need them. He wrapped his arms around X'ah from behind, breathing into his ear like a lover. "She is right, you know. I *am* stronger than you. You will always be here for them, but so will I. Despair is strong, but Hope is stronger."

X'ah screamed, lashing out at the girl, but his tentacles bounced off of her like she was under glass. Then he lashed back at Jesse, who calmly ignored the tentacles tearing at him. X'ah kept striking, and pieces of flesh and clothing were flayed from Jesse's back. But Jesse didn't appear to notice. He leaned in, and seemed at first to be kissing X'ah on the neck, but his mouth kept opening wider, and he drew X'ah in, slurping the demon's grotesque form into his mouth, slurping the tentacles in last.

He turned to the screaming demons. "Be gone," he said, and they were.

The girl wrinkled her nose at him. "You *ate* him. *Yuck.*"

"It was *yuck*. He tasted awful."

The girl laughed. "I have to go find Mama."

Jesse nodded. He turned and found his guns, slung them in their holsters. He patted his stomach, and opened a door to nowhere. "Come, father, we should get you home."

The Under-dweller

"What are we doing here, boss?" Jackson asked.

Sam shifted where he sat propped up against the mine's wall and grinned over his cigarette at the others. "Only one way in, only one way out: you do the math."

"Jesus, Sam," Ryan snapped. "The bastard's got to be bleeding to death if he ain't dead already. Tim put three holes in him, and we've dogged him for nearly twenty miles tonight. He probably came here to hide and die in peace."

Anger filled Sam's eyes as he got to his feet. "It wasn't your wife he murdered, so I will only ask you once to shut the hell up." Sam's hand crept towards the revolver holstered on his hip. "I said, we're gonna stay right here until we know for sure he's dead."

"And how are you going to know that?" Ryan argued back, getting to his feet, too. "We gonna wait here forever? I, for one, sure ain't going down in there looking for him."

Sam spat out his cigarette at Ryan's boots. "Tim'll go with me even if the rest of ya'll are too yellow. Ain't that right Tim?"

Tim sat in the corner of the entrance to the mine, rocking back and forth like a child as he hummed to himself. He held the picture of a beautiful woman in his hands, staring at it. Despite the twin silver pistols he wore on his belt, he looked innocent and lost in a world of his own.

Though Tim didn't answer, Sam turned back to Ryan and Jackson. "See, I told you. Tim is with me to the end. He's a good son."

For a moment, the only sound inside the mine's entrance was Tim's quiet humming. Then Jackson spoke: "Guess I'd best go see to our horses. Don't want no one makin' off with 'em while we're down there."

"You do that," Sam ordered in a cold, heavy voice. "What about you Ryan? You in or out?"

Ryan glanced at Tim before looking back at Sam. "I'm in, Samuel . . . But I want you to know I am doing this for Tim and his mother, not you."

"Don't matter to me none," Sam answered, taking a flask of whisky from his jacket pocket and unscrewing the top, "as long as what needs doing gets done." He took a hit off the whisky and replaced the flask. "We'll head down into the mine as soon as Jackson gets back."

When Jackson returned, he found Sam and Ryan preparing torches. It was dark outside as the night had settled in, and the only light came from an ancient lantern hanging on the wall of the mine. Sam had somehow managed to get the antique working.

Sam lit a torch and thrust it at Jackson. "Here. You and Ryan carry the lights. Tim and I will do the shooting."

"Doubt there'll be any call for that," Jackson laughed. "Like Ryan said, Tim got him pretty good."

Sam walked over to Tim and gently placed a hand on his son's shoulder. "Tim? Tim, it's time to go."

Tim stopped humming. He carefully tucked away the photo of his mother and followed the others down into the darkness of the tunnel. They walked for what seemed like hours until they reached the first intersection. The shaft broke off into a series of passageways.

"Shit!" Sam cursed. "What the hell are we supposed to do now?"

"We could split up," Jackson suggested, "leave someone here to watch the way out. We'd cover a lot more ground that way."

Tim moaned. Ryan turned to look at him and saw blood staining the boy's blonde hair and running down his face. Ryan rushed to his side and saw that the blood wasn't Tim's. Tim was staring at the shaft's ceiling. Slowly, Ryan and the others looked up, too. Gagging, Jackson cupped a hand over his mouth. Sam quickly averted his eyes, and Ryan dragged Tim out from underneath the body that bled above them. There was no question in any of their minds. It was Hank, the man who had killed Sam's wife. Most of his skin had been flayed away, and his scalped head dangled at an odd angle. Four large metal spikes, one through each of his arms and legs, pinned his body to the rock above. A fifth stake protruded from the center of his chest.

"Oh Lord, forgive us," Jackson muttered.

"For hell's sake, we didn't do that!" Sam shouted. "I wanted him dead, but not like—Jesus, not like *that*."

"I think the question we should be asking here, boys," Ryan interjected, "is who *did* do it?"

"*Him,*" Tim said, and they all froze.

From one of the side passageways, a man stepped into the torchlight, only he wasn't a man at all. His hair was long like an Indian's, and he was dressed in the tattered remains of what could have once been clothing. The man's skin swam. It was like a black fluid swirling over his bones, often exposing their whiteness in patches. Yellow teeth gleamed wetly in his snarling mouth.

Tim's hands were a blur. Everyone thought that Tim was crazy, an idiot (he'd been shot in the head during the war with the Mexicans), but no one had the nerve to say anything to his face. Off in the head or not, the boy knew how to kill. His six shooters clapped off a series of bursts before any of the other men even had time to move. Each of Tim's bullets struck its target. The black-fluid man staggered under the onslaught, then the mine was quiet again as Tim's guns clicked empty over and over again.

The thing straightened up and opened its outstretched palm towards them. In its hand rested Tim's bullets. The creature titled its head to one side, studying them as would an animal.

Jackson ran without looking back. Ryan tossed aside his torch, taking aim at the thing with his rifle. Sam had already drawn his revolver and had opened fire. Tim merely stood there with his guns leveled at the monster, clicking empty as he continued to pull the triggers. *"Him,"* Tim moaned again.

Jackson heard gunshots behind him, then screams. He ran out of the mine and into the starlight, falling to his knees. He nearly screamed himself as he noticed the skull stuck on top of a stake in the ground, half-buried in the bushes outside the shaft's mouth. There were Indian words scribbled on it in some kind of dried red substance. He understood it to be a warning of some kind, but the only word he knew enough Indian to make out was "Under-dweller." He leapt back to his feet and raced to where he'd left the horses. He felt bad about leaving Mr. Samuel and the others, but he was getting the hell out of there and was never coming back.

Lucy

"Oh lord," Jefferson muttered. "It took his eyes!"

Captain Peter's corpse lay on the floor of the bridge below him. Shane could see from the telltale bruising around the Captain's neck that it had crushed the bones inside, which had been the *real* cause of Peter's death. Jefferson squatted beside Peter's remains, on the verge of a breakdown. Shane yanked the younger man to his feet. "Pull your shit together right now, Private!" he ordered, staring Jefferson in the face. "We've got to get off this station before it gets us, too, and your bawling ain't gonna help us do that, now is it?"

Jefferson shuddered but seemed to calm down a bit. "I didn't sign on for this shit."

"Neither did I," Shane answered grimly as he checked the charge level in his pulse rifle. "How are you doing on ammo?"

Jefferson checked his own weapon. "I got about four shots."

"Then let's hope to God that's all you'll need." Shane led the way off the bridge.

"Where are we going, Sarge? The thing fired all the escape pods, and there isn't any other way off the station."

At least part of that statement was true. The thing had managed to get into engineering and reroute the power from the core to generate a massive EMP through most of the station's system, including the emergency life-pods, all before anyone realized just how smart the creature had already gotten. It was only by a miracle that life-support had somehow stayed working. Shane shook his head. Two days ago, the thing had only been a blob of genes in a test tube, and now it was an adult and a demon on two legs. There had been twenty-three people aboard the station, most trained officers, and today there was only himself and Jefferson. The creature had picked them all off, one at a time.

Shane raced down the corridor with Jefferson tromping along behind him. "No," he called back over his shoulder. "There is one other way off the station, and it knows it, too."

Shane reached the level's maintenance tube and ripped off its cover. He hopped onto the ladder inside and started to climb upwards. He just hoped they would reach the docking level before it did.

Minutes later, Shane and Jefferson stood outside the sealed entrance to the dock, one of them on each side of the massive blast door. Shane started to type in the last digit of the unlocking code and glanced over at Jefferson. "You ready?"

The young man nodded. Shane hit the last number and they leapt inside, rifles at the ready. Shane had expected the thing to be here, waiting on them, but the room appeared empty except for the station's sole shuttlecraft. Jefferson stared at it. "What good is that going to do us? The Captain was the only one—"

"Who could use it," Shane finished for him.

"Hello, boys," a voice from the shadows spoke. "Looking for these?" Naked, drenched in blood that was not her own, she stepped out of the darkness, still managing to look more beautiful than an angel. In her outstretched palm, she offered them Peter's eyeballs.

Jefferson screamed and jerked up his rifle. He fired, but she was already gone when the blue energy scorched the wall where she had stood.

Shane watched as she seemed to materialize beside Jefferson. Her clenched fist entered through Jefferson's back and burst through the front of his chest. Blood poured from Jefferson's mouth with a horrible gargling noise as he continued to scream.

Project Rebirth was a startling success. Shane had to admit that. Too bad the assholes in the white coats had brought back the wrong divine being, and with gender issues to boot.

Shane took a step back. "Lucy, Lucy, Lucy," he said, pointing his rifle at her. "You got one hell of a temper, girl." He squeezed the trigger, and bolt after bolt struck the advancing creature, burning away its flesh. Lucy knocked the weapon from Shane's hands and lifted him effortlessly into the air.

"Just wait until I get back to Earth. Being stuck in an incorporeal limbo for a few thousand years thanks to some fool dying on a cross is enough to piss anyone off."

With that said, she ripped out Shane's still-beating heart and tossed it across the room. Lucy only stopped long enough to recollect Peter's eyes, which she used for the shuttle's ID scan before heading for the ship, humming happily. A whole new era and Earth awaited her return. She hoped that the people there would be able to guess her name.

The More Things Change

"Mary, Mary?" Xander called as he crept through the main room of the inn. "Where are you?" Corpses lay all around him. Some lay sprawled on the floor, bullet holes covering their flesh like sores. The streets outside were no different. Xander had known it would be crowded here; he hadn't imagined just how crowded. The death toll didn't matter to him though. She had to die tonight. And there was no turning back.

Xander had used up all the ammo he'd brought with him and had discarded his twin UZIs and his 9mm. All he had left was his microfilament blade, which was shaped like a machete and designed to cut through steel with a single stroke. No need for that here though. Everything in the inn was so primitive it made him sick. Tomorrow, when the bodies started to stink, he imagined they could only begin to smell better than the unwashed masses they were now. Decay, at least, was an odor to which he was accustomed.

Out of the corner of his eye, Xander noticed the innkeeper and turned to admire his own handy work. The innkeeper had been one of the last to be slaughtered, and Xander had nailed him to the inn's wall, slowly cutting off his flesh in sections as the man had screamed and denied knowing anyone by her name. Xander smiled at the memory. He'd known Mary was here all along. This was where she was supposed to be, this place, so he had taken his time and had had some fun. Xander knew the witch couldn't run far, alone in her current state, but he cursed himself now. When he went out to the stables after her, she hadn't been there, and so he'd come back here. It was the only place she could've made it to.

If he could just kill her, he'd be free of his deal at last. He alone would sit at the master's right hand, where he belonged, and not burn in the lake with the other soul-sellers and sinners.

A muffled cry of pain came from outside the inn. Xander's head jerked up. "Mary?" he called, moving towards the inn's rear entrance. "Is that you?" He stepped out onto the dirt street and smiled. Though her clothes were torn and her face was caked with dust and blood, he knew it was her instantly. She was trying to crawl away, to escape, despite her obscenely bloated stomach. A trail of blood stretched out behind her, marking her path.

Xander walked over and looked down at her. "You shouldn't have let yourself get knocked up by that angel, babe," Xander laughed. Mary looked up at him as if she hadn't understood what he had said but the fear in her eyes spoke volumes. Xander reached out with the end of his blade, positioning it under her chin. "Where is your God now, woman?"

"He may not be here," a voice called from behind Xander, "but I am." The assassin turned to see a young man barely older than Mary herself, dressed in a temporal police uniform and pointing a pistol at him. The night lit up as the pistol flashed three times.. The first severed Xander's hand, and his blade thudded to the ground. The second spilt his intestines onto the sand. The final shot streaked through his face as he toppled over, nearly headless.

The young man stepped over Xander's remains and offered his hand to Mary. "Sorry I couldn't be here earlier, ma'am. My name is Officer Joseph. Don't you worry now; history is still on track just fine. Let's get you back into the stables. It's time."

Mary cried out as another contraction ripped through her. Joseph helped her to her feet, and they stumbled off together. The North Star lit the sky above them.

Hell's Daycare

They met online, of course. Jay's lack of personal hygiene pretty much precluded him from engaging in all but the simplest and most necessary social excursions. Still, visually he wasn't an unappealing sort of fellow. When he donned his ratty stovepipe hat and battered spectacles, which were missing an arm and which rested on the bridge of his nose, he almost put one in mind of Gary Oldman's translation of Dracula—if one were viewing him over a web cam, which one would have been when he was in that get-up. Up close and personal, his hirsuteness put him closer to the wolf-kin than the vampyr.

Jay adjusted the web cam, focusing it on the three-quarter view of his head that included the armed side of his spectacles; he then began trolling the Goth Camgirl's site. Having worn out his welcome with the standard fare, he started with the "new links" page. At first, he was disappointed, as the new links weren't all that new—most were simply old faces with new names—but then one picture caught his bespectacled eye. The picture was a still shot, announcing that "Succubus" wasn't there at present, but would be on at midnight, PST—fifteen minutes. Her portrait though, above the text, caused him to gasp.

She wasn't vampiric, or even Gothic. She was blonde, of all things, with little make-up and a lot of natural beauty. She appeared innocent and a little frightened, and she appealed to his predatory nature immediately. Even her name, Succubus, gave him a thrill, for he was "inKubus" when he ventured into the cyberspace of the night. He logged in and spent the remainder of the fifteen minutes entering his card information and drumming his fingers on the desk.

She logged in precisely at twelve and slipped on a headphone as she smiled at him. With the headphones, she looked like a telephone operator, and he stammered as he delivered his usual greeting.

"Um, good evening, Succubus. I trust you, er, rested well during the time of light?"

She smiled distractedly, "Yeah, it was okay." She leaned forward, and while she was fiddling with the volume, her ample cleavage filled the screen. Normally, this would have thrilled him, but the fact that it was an accidental shot rather than a purposeful seduction made him feel awkward, like he'd caught someone scratching herself in public. He looked away.

She leaned back. "Okay, I think that does it. What's your name, hon? Oh, inKubus, there it is. Hey, that's kinda funny, isn't it?"

He struggled to regain himself. "Yes, er, no, not funny. I think it's more like destiny. It's like we've finally found each other amongst all the poseurs and faux vampires."

She smiled warmly. "You don't like vampires?"

"Well, they're not truly the original creatures of the night, are they?"

"I suppose not, if you mean against nightmares and demons and such. Plus, you really shouldn't mix sex and blood. Gross."

"Oh," he was a little disappointed.

Suddenly she looked far from innocent, more than predatory. "And you like the sex, don't you, hon?"

He nodded weakly as his sudden arousal robbed him of his voice.

"Don't worry, baby. Mama'll take good care of you."

***

Jay woke up with the sunrise. The King of Hangovers wasn't just hammering his skull; he was practicing for the carnival, hammering hard enough to finally ring that damn bell and get the big stuffed elephant for his Queen. Jay had a vague recollection of the previous evening, and when he rubbed his head, the sudden sharp pain in his hand brought it all back. Succubus had taken him to undiscovered countries of delight and pain. There was an open blister on his hand, and he was afraid to look anywhere farther south.

He called in sick to work and spent most of the day sleeping. By the time he actually got out of bed, it was late enough to order pizza. By the time midnight came, he was almost back to normal.

"Hi there, baby. Back for more of the good stuff, are ya?"

Besides recovering, Jay had spent the evening planning ways to regain some control of the conversation, but any plans he had formulated vanished when she filled his screen. She looked, if anything, even more voluptuous tonight, her flesh a little healthier, her hair a little bouncier, her curves a little curvier.

"Um..."

"Don't worry baby, the first time's always the hardest." She brought her hands to her breasts, kneading, needing. She moaned, "Are you ready, hon?"

Jay whimpered.

***

She was right about one thing: the next day, Jay didn't feel great, but he felt good enough to go to work. And each day it got a little easier, a little more routine. He felt physically drained, but sharper, more aware. By the end of the week, he was sorting the mail at his sister's law office before the morning coffee break, finishing his duties before lunch. Which was just as well, because he'd talk his way into leaving at noon.

"Jay, you look like shit," pronounced his sister Beth.

"Yeah," echoed her partner, Martha. "You've got bags, kid, are you okay?"

"I'm fine," he said, "I've just been staying up too late."

"Well, go to bed, for God's sake," said Beth. "Dad'll kill me if he thinks I'm overworking you."

"I don't think bed is the problem," piped up Martha slyly. "Look at him. Bags under his eyes, but his acne's clearing up quite a bit—I'd say he needs to go to bed alone for a change."

Beth grinned. "Jay, you got a girl?"

"I gotta go." He fled.

"Have a good weekend!" they called after him, giggling.

That night, Succubus looked even more distracted than she'd seemed the first night. Thought distraught, she reeked of raw sexuality. She had to repeat herself three times before he could take his eyes off her and listen.

"Sorry, hon, but we gotta call it quits."

Jay was lost. "Quits?"

"Yeah, I can't see you anymore—something's come up, and I won't be around. I just wanted to say thanks and I'll see ya."

"But, Succubus, my lady, I need you. We are destined—"

"No, hon, we're not. But you'll be hearing from me, in a manner of speaking. Toodles."

She clicked off, and Jay stared blankly at the screen for an hour before he could even move. He dragged himself away from the computer and flopped into bed, tossing and turning and finally drifting off into a nightmare-filled, frustrating sleep.

About noon, an insistent knocking at his door brought him back to consciousness. Exhausted, he made his way to the door. "Yeah?"

A muffled voice on the other side said, "Delivery for inKubus."

"What?" He didn't remember ordering anything recently, and he certainly couldn't have used that name if he had.

"InKubus."

He opened the door to find a short, swarthy man standing in the hallway. The fellow couldn't have been more than four feet tall, and he wore a military or police uniform, though Jay didn't recognize the pentagram-shaped badge on his lapel. He was also wearing a three-cornered hat and was carrying a satchel full of parcels.

"You inKubus?"

"Um . . . yeah. Who's it from?"

"Couldn't tell ya. Sign here, please."

Jay did, signing his real name. Then, as an afterthought, he tagged "inKubus" on the end. "You a courier or something? I haven't seen your, um . . . " Jay stalled as the man looked up. He had a feral look and Jay chose his words carefully. "I haven't seen your uniforms before."

"More of the 'or something.'" The man looked at Jay's signature and nodded, handing him a package. "Here ya go, buddy. You've been served. Have a nice day."

He walked away while Jay examined the package. Opening it, Jay found documents that had an uncomfortable, legal familiarity. "Hey wait!"

He raced down the hallway, but the courier had vanished.

**

"It's a paternity suit." Beth frowned at the documents. "But I've never heard of Gehenna County. Must be out of state." She grinned at Jay, and Martha was smirking over her latte. "You've been holding out on me, little brother."

They were on the patio of a coffee bar, and Jay held his head in his hands. "No, I haven't. I haven't slept with anyone." He glanced up to find Martha still smirking, and added, "Recently."

Beth rolled her eyes. "Recently isn't what I'm worried about, Jay. How about six months to a year ago?"

"No."

"And the name 'Su Ccubus' doesn't ring a bell? What kind of name is that? Czech?"

"It's 'Succubus,' and no, we never slept together. That can't be her real name anyway."

"Well then, you have nothing to worry about, do you? A DNA test will clear this up in no time. Consider yourself lucky—I bet Dad wishes they had them when we were born."

"What do you mean?"

"Jesus, Jay, did you sleep through health classes entirely? Didn't you ever wonder why none of us look like each other? Or like Dad?"

"Oh."

"Anyway, there are several reasons why I can't help you: I can't practice out of state, you're my brother, and I'm criminal, not civil. I suggest you call Gehenna and get a public defense attorney. If the kid isn't yours, it'll be no contest."

"But why do I have to do this at all? I only met her last week, and I never slept with her!"

Martha finally stopped smirking and laughed outright. "That's what they all say."

***

When he opened his apartment door, Jay was assaulted by the most wonderful aroma he'd ever smelled. He couldn't place it, but it reminded him of his favorite cookies, of summer vacation and his grandmother, all rolled into one.

"Mr. inKubus?"

Jay yelped and dropped his keys as a giant glanced up at him from his kitchen table. The giant jumped, too.

"Sorry," they said in unison.

"Who are you, and why are you in my house?" Jay tried to sound intimidating, but the giant was, well . . . giant. Impossibly reclining on one of Jay's rickety kitchen chairs, he was as tall sitting as Jay was standing. Jay's voice sounded squeaky in his own ears.

The giant started again, "My name is Mr. Fravartin, and I'm your attorney."

The giant looked nervous, and Jay felt a little better. "Have you been baking?"

The giant frowned. "No. Why?"

"No reason. Go on."

The giant cleared his throat. "Well, to answer the second part of your question, I'm in your house because I thought perhaps it would be awkward to meet with you at work. Your sister is an attorney, is she not?"

"That's why you thought it would be awkward?"

"Well, yes."

"Uh-huh. And you're defending me in this paternity suit?"

Fravartin looked surprised. "How'd you know that?"

Jay sighed. "Why else would you be here? Who sent you here? Gehenna County?"

"Gosh no. I'm a Fravartin. I came directly from the Heavens. You'll be my first case."

"The Havens? Where the hell . . . never mind. Look, no offence, mister, but I'm a little weirded out by all this, and I'd like someone with a little more experience defending me."

The giant looked a little hurt and didn't say anything for a minute. Then, "Mr. inKubus?"

"The name's Jay, just please call me Jay."

"Okay, Jay. I'm the only one available for the amount of credit you have."

Jay knew he'd been late on some payments, but they'd never seized any of his cards. "Credit?"

"You know, good deeds, kind thoughts, charity. Heavenly rewards sorts of things."

"I'm not following you."

The giant stood, hunched over and filling Jay's kitchen. "And we're late."

Fravartin led Jay to the roof of the complex, where he'd parked the chariot. When Jay saw the flaming horses stamping their hooves with impatience, he began to sense that something wasn't right. "Fravartin," he said, "what the hell is going on?"

"Well, Mr. inKubus," said the giant, grasping the reins, "I mean, Jay. I'll admit that this case is sort of out of my league. I am sorry about that. Usually we defend guys who've made deals with the devil and then try to get out of them, that sort of thing." He *tsked* the flaming horses, and they lit from the roof, leaving sparks and scorch marks behind.

"This is a groundbreaking case though. It is rare, but sometimes the Succubus gets pregnant in one of her dalliances. Hasn't happened for hundreds of years, of course, but this time, Satan's talked her into suing for support. I guess he's tired of picking up the slack for so many deadbeat dads over the years."

"But I never slept with her!"

"She's a succubus, Jay. Nobody actually sleeps with her. Virtual sex is pretty well the same thing as sleeping sex, and you were awake and willing. I hate to tell you this, Jay, but I'm not defending you—there's no defense. We're just going to negotiate terms."

"How can they be sure I'm the father?"

"Well, they'll do the tests—there's DNA in hell, too—but she's been in reform school for quite awhile now, and swears you're the first man she ... um ... "

"Yeah."

***

The trial was over in ten minutes. Fravartin was as bad a lawyer as he seemed, and Jay didn't have anything to bargain with. Satan, who wasn't at all what Jay expected and who reminded him vaguely of Raymond Burr, was the judge. When Jay claimed that he had practiced safe sex to the best of his ability and that he hadn't even touched her, the demon prosecuting him asked if he knew what a succubus was. Jay admitted that he did, and the demon asked whether or not he knew the name of the girl who was sitting at the plaintiff's table, blushing prettily and feeding spiders to the child (it looked disturbingly like Beth) at her feet. Any thoughts he may have had about joint custody disappeared as the little bastard went from spider to table leg, constantly gnawing.

Yes, he knew her name. Could Jay please tell the court her name? He did, to titters and guffaws. It all went downhill from there.

Succubus wasn't interested in his soul—she'd had enough of that already. Satan ordered Jay to pay a figure that he'd never heard in terms of anything but budget deficits. Outside the courtroom, Fravartin fielded questions from various celestial reporters, then shuffled Jay back to the chariot.

As they took off, he said, "I'm sorry."

Jay shook himself. "Can we appeal?"

The giant laughed.

"I can never pay that off."

They rode back to Jay's apartment in silence. When he dropped Jay off, Fravartin handed him a small silver coin. "For luck," he said, and rode off into the sky.

***

The next payday, Jay stormed into Beth's office. "What is this, a tip?"

She shrugged. "I'm sorry, little brother. We received some very legal documents that say we have to garnish your wage."

He collapsed into a chair, beaten. "How about I become a contract worker?"

She sighed. "I wish I could help, Jay, but this is a law office."

He bit back the snide comment and went home.

On the way, he stopped at the convenience store and picked up snacks. With literally his last dollar, he bought a lottery ticket. That night, Beth called twice, but he ignored the phone. He curled up on the couch, gorged on chips, and watched as the lottery numbers dropped, in precise order to match his ticket.

With the weirdness of the last couple of weeks, winning the lottery didn't surprise him at all. Not only that, he didn't feel the least bit hopeful. He expected something to go wrong between now and the time he collected. Either the numbers were wrong, or he'd lose the ticket—something.

Nor was he disappointed. He *did* win, and Satan's collectors allowed him to keep the decorative memento check, and not much else. He suspected a pattern was emerging.

The next few years were a blur for Jay. He spent most of his time in gambling halls, casinos, and at the track. He won the lottery often enough to be investigated by every gaming commission in the state. Proprietors of the gaming establishments he frequented invited him for dinners and heated personal conferences regularly. But because he never had a cent to show for any of his winnings, even the thugs had nothing to pin on him and eventually left him alone.

The first time he overheard some one mutter "deal with the devil," as he raked in a phenomenal pile of chips, he got up and punched the man square in the face.

He occasionally saw his son; he had become a lawyer for Beth, who was now a senior partner.

After more years of macaroni and cheese and cheap beer, he finally realized that the only way out of his dilemma was the permanent one. He stood atop a bridge, leaning out over the dark waters and waiting for his life to flash by.

"Fravartin," he said, and the giant was there.

"Jay," he nodded.

"Is it true about suicides not going to heaven?"

"I don't know."

"Oh. Well, here's your quarter. Thanks, it was lucky. Hang around for a bit, will you?" And he stepped off.

***

Jay opened his eyes, and she was there.

"Hiya, baby."

He smiled. "Our boy's doing okay, huh?"

"Who? Oh yeah. Listen, I'm supposed to show you your room."

He followed her and thought, *Well, I guess that was right.*

She led him through a pastel-colored hallway, decorated with random crayon drawings of tortured souls, the kind of art Van Gogh or Munch might have painted in kindergarten.

"Where are we?"

"It's your new job. It's sort of a reward, I thought. I mean, little Cambion is all grown up and pretty self-sufficient, and it really doesn't seem fair that you should have to support me still, now that you're, you know, dead and all."

She opened a door and led him into a room filled with children. They looked up at him expectantly, hungrily. She continued, "I thought since you did such a good job working to support us before, you might like the chance to work directly with some of the little bastards, here at the source."

She turned to the young demons in training. "Children, this is Mr. inKubus. He's going to be your substitute for the next several centuries while Mr. Satan is away. Don't maim him too much."

Jay flashed a weak smile to the group and nervously started to write his name on the chalkboard.

Last One Standing

"Line 'em up."

The bartender greeted us with the familiar battle cry of the working day's end as the four of us entered Spuds, a shitty little tavern with wood-paneled walls, a couple of dartboards, an off-kilter pool table, and peelers every fourth Saturday. It suited us just fine.

"Well, boys, hot enough for ya?" Mario was the only Mexican that stayed in Emperor year-round, and he enjoyed the old jokes, the lame one-liners, and the fact that we still worked in the orchards and he didn't. He'd got out and started working in this little hole twenty years ago, and the old man who'd owned it had willed it to him. Six years ago, it became Spuds instead of Frank's. Don't ask me why.

"It is a hot one today, señor," I answered him, reaching for the beer and grinning. He grinned back, and we shared the same tired joke.

Me and the boys raised our bottles, and the new kid (Dave, we'll call him) he asked, "Last one standing?"

We all nodded, "Drinks for free." We all put forty bucks on the bar, and Mario whisked the money into the tip jar behind him, which was just a formality. We all knew I wasn't paying. I hadn't paid for a drink in twenty years.

The bar started to fill up within minutes of our arrival. Most of the guys coming in were other pickers, and there were a few locals, who, like us, worked for shit money and pissed most of it away. It was one of those kinds of towns.

Occasionally tourists would drop in, but they didn't usually stay long. We weren't rude to them or anything, and Mario certainly welcomed everybody's cash, but in little bars like this, there is an unspoken exclusivity that'll put a country club to shame.

I've lived in Emperor for almost thirty years. I grew up in a town just like it, in the Imperial Valley of California. I pulled carrots alongside my dad's migrant workers until I had enough money to think about college. Then I used that money to get out before they came to pick me up for the army.

My brother Jack had gone to Vietnam in '68, came home in '70, minus his hands. The dad-imposed patriotism didn't survive against the stories that Jack told me about friendly fire and the rumors he'd heard about stuff like Agent Orange, so when my traveling orders came in '71, I split town.

I headed for Canada, of course, and goofed off in Vancouver for a while, which was, and to a large degree still is, the San Francisco of Canada. Eventually, I needed money and the opportunity to spend the summer someplace where it didn't rain all the time, which brought me to Emperor, BC, in the south of the Okanogan. The winters were bitch cold, and the summers were stinking hot, but not as hot as home. Everything else was hauntingly like home. It felt familiar and comfortable, and I just hadn't gotten around to leaving.

I drove a cab in the winter and picked fruit in the summer. It was hard, hot work, and if you've never done it, there is no way I can make you understand it. It's one of those grimy jobs that immigrants do because spoiled white kids won't. One of those jobs that your dad says builds character.

I was easily the oldest guy in the orchards, and I probably could have found something else, as long as I'd been there, but I never got around to it. I think it had something to do with running away from the army. The patriotism didn't die when I split, but I was scared, and I didn't want to die for something useless. That war was different, and the people in it weren't the heroes that drank with Dad at the Vets Club.

So I compensated by punishing myself, I guess. I worked harder, played harder, and drank harder than anyone, and no one questioned my manhood but me. I'd lived in Emperor for five years by the time Carter pardoned us, and I gave him a "fuck you" with a tequila shot while I watched it on the news.

Martin and Luis were shooting pool, trying to take the table away from some buddies, when Dave looked at me like he knew something I didn't. He was the new kid in the orchards, had started halfway through the season, and so far none of us was going to make any money on our odds of how long he'd last. If he made it to the end of the season, only three weeks away, we'd tell him about the bet, and give him the money.

He was a good kid, but no more inclined to tell me his story than I was to tell him mine. Fine by me. We shot the shit and watched TV for a while (Mario and I liked the *beisbol*, and had never taken much to hockey) when Dave flashed that grin again. He looked at Mario and asked, "Hey, Mario." He pronounced it *Mare-ee-o*, like in Andretti; in Canada, it's *Mare-ee-o, tăco, drăma*. "You got any Jager? Me and Jim are thirsty."

Mario glanced at me, and I rolled my eyes.

***

Three weeks later, with me no poorer, we celebrated the end of the season. Most of the guys were heading south after a few days of shopping and buying presents for their families. At the U.S. border, they'd get busted by *la migre* and get a free ride to the Mexican border. From there, they were on their own.

At Spuds, it was a massive going away party, as well as a coming of age for Dave. He'd earned his spurs, or stripes, or whatever, and laughed with the rest of us when we told him about the bet. He could afford to be a good sport—he'd just earned a couple hundred bucks.

He bought the first round, which left him with about half, and then we established last one standing. Mario waved us over. I called Martin and Luis.

We stood at the bar, and Mario said, "You four are always the first ones in and the last ones out. Like soldiers."

I winced, but they didn't notice.

"I have a special reward for you compadres, though you might find the honor doubtful."

"Dubious," Dave muttered.

Mario pulled a bottle from under the bar. He was being mysterious, which made me smile. The bottle was tall, and I thought at first it was green, but that was the liquor. Mario grinned as he showed us that he was cracking it—it was as virgin to us as we were to it. The label looked old-fashioned; it said said, "Absente."

"What you got here, amigo?" I drawled.

"This, my friends, is a reward given to me by the liquor lady. She came this spring, and like every year, she gave me a bottle. But this year is special."

I laughed. "Special how? Because we're her test-market?"

He looked abashed, but continued his snake oil show. "This is Absinthe, Jaime, favored by the wise."

"Bullshit. Absinthe's illegal. And poisonous."

He shook his head. "No. The liquor people have refined it, used less poisonous wormwood. No more poison, but still absinthe. Still can kick your ass."

The others roared with laughter. We'd gathered quite a little crowd now, and Mario warmed to his performance. "It's still a little bitter," he said, and pulled out a spoon and some sugar.

Most of these young guys had never even heard of absinthe, but when Mario called it *ajenjo* there was a general murmur.

I read the bottle while he answered questions. The label confirmed what he said, that essentially, this was absinthe. It had been refined, but still used traditional recipes and brewing methods. And it was fifty-five percent alcohol, stronger than most stuff you can buy here.

"What's it say, Jim?" asked Dave.

"It's an herbal thing, kid. Like Jager." I laughed, and he blushed.

Mario was busy now. He had poured sugar into a tablespoon and was holding it over a lighter. The bit with the spoon put my mind to forbidden things, dangerous things. He was the consummate showman.

He took the bottle from me as soon as the sugar had caramelized and poured double shots over the sugar into five ice-filled highball glasses. He set the spoon aside and pushed glasses at Dave, Martin, Luis, and me. He took the last one himself and sighed, his performance complete.

"Everybody ropes," he said.

"And everybody rides," we answered, and we drank.

The taste was interesting, kind of sweet and bitter at the same time, but not bittersweet. I don't know, it's hard to explain, even now. There was a general disappointment in the crowd when none of us immediately keeled over. After a couple of minutes, we ordered more beers and the show was over.

We thanked Mario and talked about his new product. None of us seemed excited about it, and he was trying to decide whether or not to stock it. He had initially misjudged the popularity of Jagermeister a few years ago, and was kicking himself all through that spring break. The whole Okanogan Valley fills up with hard drinking kids from Vancouver and especially from Washington state; BC's drinking age is nineteen.

I got up to take a piss and collapsed. My knees just buckled.

There was dead silence.

"Bendejo!" Mario was around the bar and at my side in two seconds, and people started shouting. I guess it didn't occur to them I could be that drunk—they thought I had a heart attack or something.

"Jaime! Are you okay? Look at me!" Mario was yelling into my face.

"Fuck, amigo, just pick me up. I'm fine."

He did, with Martin and Dave's help, and I looked into many worried faces.

"I'm fine," I repeated, and they started to believe me. "I just slipped or something." Then I bolted for the washroom and puked up my guts.

Martin and Dave followed me, and when they saw what I was doing, Martin crossed himself. Dave laughed out loud. "Holy shit, Jim. You're pissed."

I had to agree.

They left me to my indignity, and after a couple more minutes I was done. I cleaned myself up and returned to a bar full of cheering, jeering fruit pickers. I waved and headed back to the bar.

Most of them left me alone after that, but the conversations were easily understood, even in Spanish. This was a first, and an event like this warranted much retelling. Out of the corner of my eye, I saw a few demonstrations of how my feet had failed me, for the benefit of those who hadn't actually seen it, or maybe just for the hell of it.

"You okay, Jaime?" Mario asked again.

"Yeah, guess I'm getting old. Gimme a beer." This was weird, and it scared me. I don't know if it was my Scottish ancestry, or just hard living, but I had never had anything like that happen before. Sure, I got drunk, don't get me wrong. But I had never had the blackouts, never collapsed. I had certainly never puked.

Dave was all over this one.

"Man, Mario, that is some wicked kind of brew you got back there. Knocked ol' Jim right on his ass, eh?"

Mario was still watching me, concerned.

"I mean, shit, flat on his face, and puking like a punk rocker. Wham, bam, thank you—"

"Enough, Dave," said Mario.

"It's okay, amigo. He can ride me a bit. Where's that beer?"

Mario slid me a cold one, and Dave took my last remark as license to kill.

"So this is how the mighty fall out here in the sticks, eh? Man, Jimbo, looks like we finally found your kryptonite. Or maybe you're right. Just getting old, eh? We'll have to slap a nipple on your bottle this time next year."

I turned to him. "My name is still Jim, kid. You can't manage that, just say 'sir.'"

He got kind of a mean look then. "Shit, Jimbo. If I knew I could have seen a performance like that, I'd have left Calgary years ago. Gonna be fun watching you get senile."

I hadn't been in a fight in probably fifteen years. When I first started living and working among the other pickers, I had had to establish myself. Usually, I could talk my way out of a fight and just out drink them. But not all the time. I didn't win every fight, but I always gave somebody something to remember. After a few years, it just wasn't necessary anymore.

I had been around so long now that I was a fixture, and, along with Mario, I carried a certain amount of authority in the transitional community. But Dave was new, and he wasn't here out of choice. He was on the run, like me. I knew that. Maybe he thought it was time for a new old man.

He was wrong. And in about two minutes, I showed him how wrong he was.

It took Martin, Luis, and a couple others to pull me off him, and I didn't calm down until Mario called me by name. The haze cleared, and the smug look, along with a fair amount of skin, had been wiped off Dave's face. He was a mess.

"Jaime, what the hell?"

"I don't know, amigo. I really don't. Last thing I remember, the kid was mouthing off."

"Si, and then you tried to kill him."

I looked at him—he was serious. If somebody had asked me who beat the shit out of the kid, I honestly couldn't have told you.

"Jaime," said Martin, "he's not breathing."

"Shit."

"Put him in the back. Come on." Mario led the three guys, dragging Dave to the back. They put him in the storeroom, and a couple of guys got him breathing again. They let him sleep.

Mario handed me a fresh beer.

"No," I said, and pointed to the bottle of absinthe.

"Jaime…"

We stared at each other for a moment, then he poured us each another.

"Salud."

It went down easier this time, tasted better. And I wasn't sick.

***

Dave died later that night, and Martin, Luis, and I threw him in the lake, minus his wallet and his winnings. They found him a few days later, well after the workers had gone home. Turned out he'd killed his girlfriend in Calgary, along with the guy she'd been screwing. Same old story and nobody was real concerned with finding out who'd robbed and killed him. They blamed the workers, of course, and several would be questioned next year, but the Mounties didn't figure the killer would come back anyway.

That night, I dreamed. A woman came to me, and my brain called her Mario's liquor rep, though I'd never met her. She was dressed in a tight green sweater, and she thanked me for saving her honor from Dave. Then, we fucked like minks.

***

Fall came, and I got my job as a cabbie again. It was a slow time, most of my business coming from the airport in Kelowna, taking suits to hotels, making good tips by recommending the best peeler joints.

I still hung out at Spuds when I wasn't in the city, though it wasn't nearly as busy this time of year. Strictly the locals, no strippers. We didn't discuss that night— Mario never gave any indication that he still had the bottle, and I didn't ask. We watched baseball till November, then football till January. We didn't talk much.

I thought about that night though. I thought about killing that kid, and I thought about the things he'd said before I had. Somehow over the years, I'd become alpha wolf, and it wouldn't be long before some other pup stepped up to the plate.

Mostly though, I thought about absinthe.

I wondered what it was that had knocked my knees out from under me. I'd had stronger drinks before. We were right on the border, and it wasn't hard for the guys to bring moonshine up, 190 proof, stuff that, after you drink it, leaves a film in the glass that burns for a full minute. Shine had never done to me what this stuff did, if that's what it was.

One night, I had a fare from the airport, a suit from the States, up doing sales in the ass end of his territory. He invited me into the hotel lounge for a drink. I think he was lonely, and my accent still gives me away from time to time.

We had a couple of beers, chatted inanely about his shitty life for a while, and when he invited me up to his room for another drink, I finally clued in. It took me by surprise, but it didn't offend me. Hell, it'd been a while since anybody found me interesting enough to sleep with.

I didn't know what to say, until he asked, "Have you ever had absinthe?"

Cold sweat broke out on my forehead. "No," I stammered, "look, I'll come up for a drink, but nobody can see me, okay?"

He understood that, all right. "Of course. Knock in ten minutes."

I thanked him for the drinks loudly, and left. I made sure I squawked the tires on the way out of the parking lot. I pulled around the corner and parked behind the mechanic's shop. I waited five minutes, wondering what the hell I was doing, then snuck back to the motel. Nobody saw me go up to his room.

I knocked, and he answered, quickly ushering me in. He didn't want me to be seen either. Good.

He poured us drinks, and I watched as it swirled around the glass in slow motion as he poured it. I sat in a chair, by the TV, and he sat on the edge of the bed. He was nattering about something, but I just stared into my glass.

"I'm going to have a shower."

"Yeah."

He looked like he didn't expect me to be there when he came out. I don't blame him.

I sniffed the drink, looked at the bottle. It wasn't the same brand—this stuff was a bit stronger, but also called itself "Absente."

I downed mine, and stood up immediately.

My legs wobbled a bit, and I felt awful. I headed for the bathroom.

I want to get one thing straight right now. I didn't kill this suit because he was gay, or because he was hitting on me. I'm not some kind of racist or homophobe with a perverted justice complex. There's no deep-rooted reason in my psyche for what I've become, apart from plain old selfishness. Hell, it wasn't like I hadn't slept with men before—any port in a storm.

I got into the bathroom, heading for the toilet, and he said, "Hey, are you okay?"

"No." I could feel it in me, like a fucking poker in my chest, and my brain stem was on fire. But I turned away from the toilet and ripped back the curtain.

"Hey!"

I gave him a shove, and he lost it completely, taking a tumble and whacking his head on the edge. He was groggy, but not out. I grabbed his head and hit it on the bottom again. He was out.

The sickness in me disappeared, the fire in my brain lashing out along my nervous system as I jammed the heel of his foot into the drain. The tub started to fill, and I turned his head.

As he began to drown, he started to come out, but I held him down, and his struggles eventually faded.

I was on fire. I watched him die. His nerve impulses moving along his naked body had slowed down enough and had become large enough that I could watch as they sped along, running back and forth from his brain to his extremities. Or else my perception was heightened enough to see them. Whatever.

He died, and I could see his soul leave the body. I was a fucking god.

Gradually, I came back to myself and realized what I'd just done. It was horrible, and I should have felt awful, but my guilt was a tangible thing, a piece of my soul that I could detach from the rest, look at, and put in my pocket.

I went back to the other room and had another glass. I left the half bottle there, tempted as I was to take it, then I took my own glass with me and left.

***

The paper talked about a visiting businessman dying in a freak tub accident, and those that did comment on it cracked jokes. The poor bastard would get laughed out of hell.

I dreamed that night. I was being court-martialed. Dad was there, and he was weeping. That gave it away, and I knew it was a dream before I woke up.

***

The next night, I stopped into Spuds. Mario was watching a hockey game and counting beer.

"What the hell, Mario? Nothing else on?"

He grinned at me. "I got money on this one."

"Ah."

We watched the game for a bit, then without taking my eyes from the TV, I asked, "Mario, what do you know about the *ajenjo*?"

He didn't look at me either. "I wasn't joking when I said it was the drink of the wise, amigo. All the heavyweight artist types drank it, sung its praises. It was supposed to give visions, stuff like that. It made Van Gogh crazy. It's been around forever, but the recipe has changed over the years."

"Van Gogh, huh?"

"Yup. Picasso, Hemingway, all those guys."

"What do you mean it's 'changed'?"

"In the old days, it was just wine infused with wormwood, like they do with fruit now. Then in the 1800s, they started mixing and distilling pure herbs, hallucinogenic ones. There was an old brujo in my town who used to drink it, along with shrooms and peyote"

"Was he any good?"

"As a brujo?" I could see him nod out of the corner of my eye. "He was. Crazy as a shithouse rat, though."

I turned to look at him. "How do you know all this stuff?"

He looked at me like I was an idiot. "I'm a bartender."

***

The next weekend, I cleaned myself up and took a flight to Vancouver. I'd saved a bunch of money over the years, had always thought of getting my own little orchard one day. Now, I was getting bored with the Okanogan. There was a lot of world out there to see, and I was tired of hiding from it.

The fact that I'd killed two people in the last few months didn't really register most of the time. It was there, sort of a point of reference in my psyche, but it was detached from my conscience. After thirty years of stagnation, my mind was ready for some meat.

I took a cab from the airport to downtown. It was raining of course. I got a room at one of the old fancy hotels, where you get a mint on the pillow and fresh towels on the hour. I went down to the lounge to check things out.

The nice thing about Vancouver is that you can look like shit and still get great service at the poshest places. Very democratic—if you have the money, you're in. Thing is, there's a lot of movie people there. It's a great location city and cheap to film in. So no matter how bad you look, you might be somebody, and no waiter in the world is going to blow the opportunity for a great tip or for the chance to be discovered.

I didn't look like shit, but close. The lounge was dressed like an old boys' club, thick leather chairs and faux antiques. The bookshelves were full, and the books were dusty.

I grabbed a seat at the bar, was immediately pounced upon by a young wavy-haired bartender. Before he could speak, I said, "Gin and tonic," and unfolded the newspaper I'd brought down from the room.

He pouted, but started making my drink.

I heard a snort from the end of the bar, and glancing that way, I saw a girl about twenty-five or so hiding a grin behind her hand. I grinned back and returned to my paper.

The bartender brought my drink and vanished, whereupon the girl down the way got up and plunked herself beside me. "I've never seen Kevin get shot down like that before. He didn't even get a chance to flatter you."

I looked up. She was cute, freckled, though I thought she could stand to eat a bit more. Her eyes had a lot of mischief in them. She was wearing the dark pants and dress shirt, but she had a jacket on. I smiled at her and didn't think about my age.

"Are you off work now, or on a break?"

"I'm off. You going to buy me my next drink?"

I thought about giving her a smart-ass reply about this being modern times, but stuck with my old-fashioned ways. "Sure."

We sat for a moment, wondering where to go, and then I said, "Should I apologize to Kevin?"

"Hell, no," she smiled. "I get tired of hearing him. Let him suffer."

"My name's Jim."

"Sandy," she gave me nice firm handshake. "And so you're new in town. But you've been here before."

I was impressed. "Okay, I give. What gave me away?"

She shrugged. "My secrets. But I also deal in a casino if that makes you feel any better."

I laughed. "It does."

To cut to the chase, I took her upstairs. I don't know if she thought I was somebody or if she just liked old guys. I checked with Kevin, and sure enough, they stocked two kinds of absinthe; it had been getting popular with the movie-types. I took a bottle with us and she laughed.

"You like that shit?"

"Don't you?"

"I haven't tried it yet. I'm not big on trendy things. I like beer."

"Just wait."

In my room, I burned some sugar the way Mario had done, but then I mixed it in. We had a glass and went to bed.

I don't know who started it, but it was rough. Rough, hell, it was like she'd had the Marquis de Sade for a kindergarten teacher. It was new for me, and she took great satisfaction from seeing my startled, then pleased looks, over and over. I learned a lot that night, and whether the drink inspired the depravity, or the other way around, I'm not sure.

I left her sleeping, a devious little smile on her lips, while I got up and poured a glass straight. I watched the rain and drank, appreciating the beauty of the city at night. From up here, there was no noise, and the mist captured and held the lights, covering the streets with a luminescent dome. In the distance, I could see the lights from Grouse coming down the ski hill like a starry trail.

I must have dozed, because I dreamed.

Jack was there, grinning at me. "So my little brother's finally growing up."

"Growing up, hell. I'm older than you got." The last time I called home, Dad had said his only son had killed himself and had hung up. The old man didn't like to waste his breath.

"Hey now, that's funny. You're a regular Tommy Smothers."

I got some glasses. "Drink?"

"Ayup."

We sat for a bit, sipping. It was a bizarre dream, in that it wasn't all that bizarre. No surreal edges or lack of focus. I figured it was more of a hallucination.

"So," I started, "I guess I'll play—what do you mean growing up?"

"Just that, Jimmy. You're not running anymore, and you're finally realizing your potential."

"For what, violence? Or alcohol?"

"Don't be a smart-ass. Do you really think this shit gets easier to drink the more violent you become?"

That was what I was starting to believe, although it didn't really make any sense.

"Of course it doesn't make sense," he answered my thought. Then he changed tacks. "Why don't we talk it out? You find a drink you can't handle until you beat somebody to death..."

"And then I drink more, and get more violent so I can drink more?"

"Kind of a stupid circle, isn't it?"

I nodded.

"What would have happened if you'd gone to 'Nam? I'll tell you. You would have lived through it, and killed a lot of people—probably some that were innocent, kids and stuff, maybe even a buddy."

"Or got killed."

He nodded. "Granted, but since you're still here now, let's suppose you were meant to live through it, but you didn't even go. So now, if you were meant to be in a certain place in your life, mentally say, you're just catching up."

"I don't know Jack, that sounds kind of far-fetched."

"So you just killed those guys for the hell of it?"

No. Not for the hell of it. Rage, the first time, and what? The desire to watch someone die, to see the process? Close enough.

"Exactly," he said. "Jimmy, do you regret them?"

"No." No false bravado—I didn't.

"Let me tell you about the guys who came home with me, or later, when the bad shit really started happening. Do you know how they made it?"

I shook my head.

"Most of them didn't. They gave up, lost hope, or were eaten up with guilt or despair. Like me. But the ones that did came to terms. They found a way to deal with their guilt, and sent despair on its way."

"Religion?" I grinned.

He nodded. "Some of them, but even that was just hiding. The ones who really survived, and excelled, learned from their shit. They accepted what they had done, accepted that they were just animals, and doing either what the leader of the pack told them, or following their instincts. And not denying them. Not now and not in the future."

I shook my head. "This sounds an awful lot like 'do what thou wilt.'"

Now he grinned. "Thelma is as Thelma does. If you prefer, how about, 'whatever gets you through the night?'" He sang it, off-key.

"You never should have gone, Jack. You were too much of a hippy."

"And *you* should have." He lifted his glass. "You know, I think this stuff was on tap at the old Hellfire club."

I heard Sandy stirring in the bedroom. "Jim?"

"You better go, little bro, and so had I."

"Wait a minute—one thing. Are you a ghost, or my subconscious playing around?"

"Does it matter?"

"Yeah, because if you're a ghost, I miss you. Goodnight."

Sandy was sitting up in bed. "Who were you talking to, Jim? Do you get voices?"

"I do now."

***

With Sandy, it was more slap than tickle, but we didn't get tired of each other. We even got to know each other. She was a fallen acolyte: she'd tried everything from Atheism to Zoroastrianism, and was still looking. We made a good pair.

We stood together outside an apartment complex in East Van, a primarily low-income residential neighborhood.

It was a long building, about four stories high and a third of the block long. We'd gone around the whole building and dowsed the eight ground-level balconies with gas, and now we waited in the alley. It was 3 AM.

"So why are we doing this?" she asked, lighting a smoke.

"See the BMW out front?" I said, and she nodded. "There's at least four cars that don't match the building—which leads me to believe that we got us some bad guys."

"So you're going to burn down the whole building to get them?"

"Yup. I want to know how it feels to kill some kids to get to the bad guys. If this were anywhere but North America, the government would be paying us to do this."

"The American government."

"How about Somalia?"

She didn't say anything.

"Does it bother you that innocent people are going to die, too?"

She shook her head and threw her cigarette. "There's no such thing,"

But she was wrong about that. As we watched the building burn, I could see the sixteen souls we sent into the night. They were different, for lack of a better term, colors. I watched them go, and tried to regret what we'd done.

"Better luck next time," I murmured.

***

We pulled a bunch of shit after the apartment building, but our violence was limited to people who pissed us off, and people who, in our blessed opinion, were polluting the gene pool. And each other. We weren't ever caught, or even looked at funny. Random crimes are really hard to investigate.

While Jack and I had decided that the magic elixir wasn't a demon, that didn't mean it wasn't magic. I thought about going to Spain, where it's still legal to get the traditional stuff. The *stronger* stuff. Besides, Hemingway had lived there, and I could do with seeing some of his old haunts.

Sandy and I were in a mall and on a whim. I dragged her to a travel agent kiosk.

"Yes, sir?" asked Mr. Smiley.

"I'm wondering what the prices are like to Spain right now."

"Oh, Spain! It's fabulous this time of year, and luckily, it's the off-season. If you can manage the heat—"

"Yeah, yeah. Just find me a decent price, okay? I already want to go."

He was taken aback—I may have lived here for thirty years, but I can still be an American when I want to.

"Of course, sir," he sulked.

He did his thing for a bit, then quoted me a couple of prices with the usual jargon, and asked, "And will you be traveling alone, sir?"

I looked at Sandy and grinned. "I hope not."

He glanced at her with a puzzled expression, then back to me. "So how many—"

"Two. One for me and one for the lady." He was starting to bug me.

"What...of course." Something was bothering him, and I was starting to get suspicious. Had he recognized her? Or me? Was he supposed to be watching for people like us trying to leave town?

He kept looking at her strangely whenever I did, and she must have sensed it, too. "I'm going to wait outside, Jim."

"Okay."

"Pardon, sir?"

"What?"

"Oh, um, nothing."

He was getting weirder, and I said, "You know what? Forget it."

I got up and went back to the mall, but Sandy wasn't around. I figured she went out for a smoke. But that wasn't right, because I always carried her smokes for her; she didn't like pockets. I looked around to see if there were security guards or cops lurking around, but nothing seemed out of the ordinary.

I went outside, and still didn't find her, so I went home, to the house we rented in East Van. Right across the street from the burned apartments, coincidentally.

***

She never came back, but I'm not surprised. Everything was getting stranger all the time, and it wasn't exactly normal when we met. I did go back to the hotel where I'd met her once, and asked if she was still working there, but they acted like they didn't know her, had never heard of her. I wondered for a second if she was even real.

Maybe it's sour grapes, but I think I outgrew her anyway.

I did some research, and started brewing my own absinthe, the old way. Wormwood isn't that hard to find if you can make friends with an herbalist in Chinatown, and the rest of the mix you can get at the market, or grow yourself. My herb garden was the envy of the neighborhood.

I also did it the really old way, with wine and wormwood, and you wouldn't believe the kick that stuff has.

***

I won't list my 'sins' for you since then. Suffice it to say that there were many. You or your God can judge me; just don't get in my way. It's good to talk about this stuff, but I actually didn't come here to confess tonight, Father. I came to get you alone in this box.

Again, I don't want you to get the wrong idea—I'm not going to kill you because of what you did to all those kids. At least, not on their behalf. I don't give a shit about them. They can deal with it and live, or whine about it and die. It's all the same to me. But personally, I find it kind of reprehensible to betray trust that way.

Quite frankly, I just don't like you.

I'll make it quick though. It's late, and I've got a busy day tomorrow.

A Madman's Ravings

I think it can truly be said that to some degree or another, anyone who writes horror in this day and age is at least in part a bit mad. The horror genre itself is almost commercially dead. Hollywood does nothing to help this by continuing to turn out films that appeal more to the teen crowd than true horror fans and it sometimes feels like horror is facing an end in our culture as the world itself becomes more and more horrific in our own day to day lives. However, I grew up reading the works of H.P. Lovecraft, watching classics like Night of the Living Dead and fun, cheesy films like Tobe Hooper's Lifeforce. I was in love with them from the moment they entered my life and I love them still. That is why I have written horror fiction and not romance, crime, or the stuff where the money lurks. Living in North Carolina, in the middle of the "bible-belt", I have faced a lot of problems from finding publishers to people "putting me down" for what I do, but it has never stopped me. I have faced my own inner demons over writing as well including lack of faith in my own work which is something every writer faces. Hack or not, I keep getting published though and it seems some people out there enjoy the nightmares I put on paper.

Madmen's Dreams is my fourth collection of short stories and is likely to be my last one for quite some time to come so I hope very much that you enjoyed it. While I do plan to continue writing though perhaps in a different medium, I have finally done what I thought was impossible and taken that step away from short fiction to longer works. My first novel, Cobble, an epic zombie tale, is due out later this year from Mundania Books and with its publication I will have achieved every goal I had when I first picked up the pen except one: to write for Marvel Comics. That is where I hope to be headed now even if it takes me years to get up the nerve to try and only the Lord knows if I will ever reach that goal or not.

Either way, *Madmen's Dreams* is, I hope, a fitting farewell to a genre that has been very kind to me. Despite all the battles and hard work, I wouldn't change a single second of the last four years of cranking out tales every week and chaining myself to my computer surrounded by gallons of coffee. And with all its varied tales from demon-filled westerns, to zombie apocalypses, to military SF, I think it is the most wide ranging thing I have ever had published as well. It was also a blast working with Mr. Pearce and a project like *Madmen's Dreams* was something the two of us had talked about for years.

All that said, keep dreaming dark dreams, keep loving those seconds when the dead surround you and you have no place to run, and thank you will all my heart for letting my nightmares be a part of those worlds inside your head.

—Eric S. Brown

About the Madmen

Eric S. Brown is a 30-year-old author living in North Carolina. He has been in love with the works of H.P. Lovecraft, Marvel Comics, and just about everything horror related— especially zombies—since he was born. He has had over 300 short stories published since March 2001. Many of these tales have collected in books including his highly praised collection *Dying Days*. His first novel *Cobble* will be published in 2005.

D. Richard Pearce is a west coast writer, and as such, may be vaguely annoying to many people. His work has appeared here and there around the web and in print, and includes individual stories, articles, and some collaborative efforts. He can be reached via his agent (read "analyst.")

It's Only Temporary
by Eric Shapiro

Earth's Last Day... What Do You Do?

After Sean graduates from college, he is ready to begin his life. Silly him for assuming he will have one. Word gets out that humanity is doomed: a giant meteorite has been headed toward the Earth for decades, and the government is ill-equipped to stop it. On the final day of human life, Sean must decide who to spend his precious time with. When he opts to hit the road and reunite with a lost love, he encounters a mad society that is rapidly shredding the trappings of civilization.

It's Only Temporary is a fevered tour of a world on fire. Throw your bookmark away; you will not be able to put this story down...

"Eric Shapiro's *It's Only Temporary* is an apocalyptic masterpiece: harrowing, hilarious, disturbing, heartfelt, and suspenseful. Not to be missed!"
—James Rollins, author of *Sandstorm* and *Amazonia*

"*It's Only Temporary* reads like a road movie travelling toward Armageddon, and its powerful, stylish writing and raw emotion will stay with you for a long, long time."
—Tim Lebbon, author of *Desolation*

"Shapiro has crafted a damn near perfect Apocalypse story in *It's Only Temporary*..."
—Michael Oliveri, author of *Deadliest of the Species*

Available July 1, 2005 from Permuted Press
www.permutedpress.com

D.L. SNELL

Hourglass

A single father braves dank mines, train tunnels and carnivorous forests, in search of the last hourglass tree, the only hope of saving his son from the deadly sting of an arachnid wasp.

"Tightens like a noose."
~C.D. Phillips, editor, *eye-rhyme*

Exit66.net/indexbooks.htm

Anthology Appearances

- **Cold Flesh,** Hellbound Books
- **The Undead,** Permuted Press
- **Monsters Ink,** Cyber Pulp
- **Mind Scraps,** Cyber Pulp

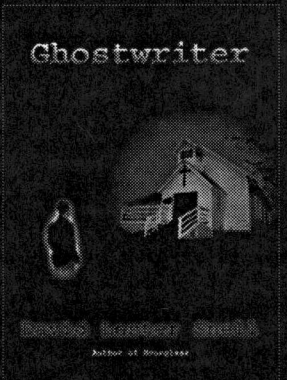

Ghostwriter

An evil priest sicks his congregation on a best-selling novelist, who relies on an un-identified entity to write his books.

"Frightful. I couldn't put it down."
~Nora Weston, author of *@hell*

Exit66.net/indexbooks.htm

THE UNDEAD

A ZOMBIE ANTHOLOGY
CONTAINING SHORT HORRORS BY
VINCE CHURCHILL, D.L. SNELL,
ERIC S. BROWN, AND MANY MORE.

Afterword by Brian Keene
Foreword by Kevin Sproles

COMING LATE 2005

PermutedPress.com

For every survivor there are more than 100,000 bodies

They don't stand a chance

Autumn
by David Moody

New book 'The Human Condition" available now

Spread the Infection

www.theinfected.co.uk